Prima Donna
By Keisha Ervin

D1595528

P.O. Box 2535

Florissant, Mo 63033

All Prioritybooks titles are available at special quantity discounts for bulk purchases for sales promotions, premiums, fund-raising, institutional or educational use. For information regarding discounts for bulk purchases, please contact Prioritybooks Publications at 1-314-306-2972 or info@prioritybooks.com. You can contact the author at: keisha_ervin2002@yahoo.com

Edited by: Lynel Washington and Kendra Koger

Cover Designed by: Sheldon Mitchell of Majaluk

Library of Congress Control Number: 2011941135

ISBN: 9780983486046

First Prioritybooks Printing: September 2011

10 9 8 6 5 4 3 2 1

Printed in the United States of America

Prima Donna
By Keisha Ervin

 Dedication

To My Dear Beautiful Son,

I have a confession to make. I wasn't sure about you at first. To me you were just this extraordinarily handsome baby that smelled nice, most of the time. When you were first born I never realized how much being a parent changes you. I don't remember the exact moment things changed; I just know that it did. One minute I was just drifting along through life, believing I was invincible. The next, my heart was beating outside of my chest, exposed to the elements of the world. Loving you has been the most profound, extreme, heart-wrenching and fulfilling experience of my life. As your mother I made a silent vow to protect you from the world. And in many ways I have failed, but I promise from this day forward that I will do better. It's me and you, Buddy, 'til the end and if don't nobody else love, you know Mommy's gonna love you 'til the end of time.

Acknowledgments

Father God, thank You for bringing me through once again. Your love and mercy are my covering and I thank You. I pray that I continue to live my life according to Your Word and not my own. Help me not to respond, but to react. Order my steps, God, and bless me to come through this trying time in my life victorious.

To my G4L girls: Locia, Tu-Shonda, Monique and Sharissa, thank you ladies for being such great friends. You all are more like sisters to me. I have really seen over the last month how much you all really and truly care for me. I couldn't have asked God to bless me with a better crew. Love you, dolls!

Mama, Daddy, Keon and the rest of the Poe and Ervin families, I love you.

Brenda Hampton, you are the best agent a girl could ask for. Over the years you have not only become my partner in crime, but a mentor and friend. You are a great remodel and I can't wait for your memoir to drop so the world can see just how blessed you are. I love you!

Mrs. Rose Jackson-Beavers, thank you once again for the opportunity to write a story for you. Working with you is always a pleasure. I wish you and your family nothing but success.

And to my loyal fans, thank you all for riding with me once again. I promise if it wasn't for y'all and me needing a paycheck I wouldn't be doing this. Your kind words of encouragement keep me going. I love each and every one of you from the bottom of my heart.

Keisha Ervin Contact Info:
    www.wix.com/kyrese99/keishaervin
    www.facebook.com/keisha.ervin
    www.twitter.com/keishaervin
    keisha_ervin2002@yahoo.com

Part One

"*I know you're mad at me, but baby, I'm so sorry.*"

Teedra Moses
"No More Tears"

A slight smile graced the corners of McKinley's lips as she rode down Washington Avenue. She couldn't have asked for a better night. The sun was setting perfectly over the horizon. Hues of orange and pink were in the sky. For a Miami spring night the temperature outside was a perfect 78 degrees. Normally, it was scorching outside, but thankfully she was able to rock the Herve Ledger iron-dust color, strapless, form-fitting bandage dress and Ruthie Davis double-platform shoetie with spikes and Swarovski crystals she'd bought especially for that night.

It was a special evening, so she had to look her best. It was April 5, her fiancé Jamil's thirty-first birthday. McKinley had an entire evening of surprises in store for him. They would attend a Heats game, but before that they'd have dinner and drinks at the ultra-exclusive restaurant B.E.D.

B.E.D, which stood for beverage, entertainment and dining was a Miami staple and located in the middle of South Beach nightlife district. Famous as a fine dining epicenter, B.E.D boasted large mattresses and mountains of pillows with the luxury of seclusion at the pull of a drape—a perfect setting for a decadent French-style cuisine with a Brazilian influence.

McKinley sat in the backseat of the Lincoln town car that Eduardo, her chauffeur for the night, drove her around in. As she checked her face, the reflection staring back at her from her Chanel compact confirmed what she'd expected. She was an absolute vision of perfection. Realizing they were getting close to the restaurant, McKinley placed her compact back inside her Judith Leiber birdcage minaudiere.

Seconds later, they pulled up to the restaurant's doors. Eduardo parked the car and hopped out to open McKinley's door. With the door opened, Eduardo leaned forward and extended his right hand.

"Thank you." McKinley placed her hand in his and stepped out.

As always, wherever she went, McKinley caused traffic to stop. All eyes were on her. Pedestrians on the street just had to catch a glimpse of the golden goddess. McKinley's distinct facial features were captivating. Everything about her was mesmerizing. She possessed brown doe-shaped eyes, deep dimples and pink pouty lips that complimented her honey-colored skin and ravenous long black hair.

She was a five-foot-four, curvy size ten. Sometimes the perception of what people thought she should be, because of her looks, was mind-boggling. McKinley constantly felt the need to stay on her "A" game. There was no way she could be caught dead in an outfit from last season or without her hair and nails done or a face beat to perfection. In Miami, looks were everything and beautiful women like McKinley came a dime a dozen.

One false move and her social status could go from the A-list to the D-list in a matter of seconds. Most importantly, chicks were dying to take her place. They craved the lifestyle Jamil showered her with and would do anything to get him in the sack. That's why that evening was so important. McKinley was determined to show him just how much she loved and appreciated him. After giving her reservation info to the maître D, McKinley was escorted to her bed, which was in the center of the room.

"Ugh," she said nervously. "Maybe this wasn't such a good idea." McKinley held onto the hem of her dress and climbed onto the bed.

Her dress was so constricting that as she scooted she lost her balance and fell forward onto her face.

"Ooh." She pushed herself back up.

"Are you all right, ma'am?" the maître D asked, stifling a laugh.

"Yeah." McKinley blew her hair out of her face, praying her makeup wasn't smeared.

"Your server will be with you shortly."

"Okay." McKinley sat on her butt and crossed her legs.

A young Puerto Rican man with curly black hair introduced himself. "Hello. My name is Juan. I will be your server for tonight. Would you like to start off with something to drink?"

"I'll just have water for right now. I'm waiting on my boyfriend to arrive. It's his birthday." McKinley smiled.

"How wonderful." The server smiled back. "I'll be right back with your drink."

"Okay," McKinley said, glancing around the restaurant.

The atmosphere at B.E.D was dope. Pink and blue lights were dimmed low to give the space a sultry Moroccan appeal. The music was pumping and drinks were being served by the dozens. Nothing but the hottest and wealthiest people surrounded her. Everyone seemed to be enjoying themselves and having a grand time.

McKinley couldn't wait for Jamil to arrive. Twenty minutes later McKinley sat on her bed alone, checking her watch, wondering where Jamil was. She'd reminded him just an hour before that they were to meet at seven on the dot. Frustrated, McKinley pulled out her cell phone and called him. He answered on the third ring.

"What up?" he said with a laugh.

"Where are you?" McKinley said low into the phone as she heard voices and music in the background.

"Hi, to you, too," Jamil shot back sarcastically.

"Where are you?" McKinley said impatiently.

"Why?"

"Ummmmm 'cause I'm sittin' at the restaurant, waiting on you. What you mean why?" McKinley shot back with an attitude.

"I'll be there in a minute."

"What's a minute, Jamil?" McKinley rolled her eyes as Jamil laughed.

"Hello?" she snapped, knowing damn well he wasn't laughing at her.

"Ay yo!" Jamil shouted to someone.

"Jamil!" McKinley raised her voice, causing people around her to stare.

"Yeah," he answered.

"Are you seriously ignoring me, and who are you talkin' to?" McKinley fumed.

"Chill out. I said I would be there in a minute," he replied sternly.

"Well, please hurry up."

"Okay, I'm leaving now."

"I'm for real, Jamil. Come on."

"I said a'ight," he huffed.

"Bye," McKinley said, ending the call.

Thirty minutes later she sat staring absently out into the crowd. *This nigga ain't coming,* she thought. Jamil had played her once again. She'd called him at least five times, but he didn't even bother to pick up. She wished she could say this scenario was all new to her, but it wasn't. Jamil's personality reminded of her Dr. Jekyll and Mr. Hyde. One minute he was this sweet, attentive man and then in the blink of an eye he'd turn into an absolute monster. With him she never knew what she was gonna get.

He'd taken her through it all. In the three years they'd been together she'd dealt with him messing around on her, his constant lies and never keeping his word. Disappointed that all of her planning and dolling herself up had been reduced to shit, McKinley placed an order to go then called Eduardo. A while after that she was home, kicking off her heels. The feel of the cold marble floor soothed her aching feet. The sight of McKinley's apartment always made her feel warm inside.

The burnt orange, tufted sectional, wooden coffee table, Nani Marquina Seagrass rug and three-panel painting by Christina Narwicz set the whole living area off right. McKinley walked into the kitchen, which was connected to the living room. The tears that had been begging to fall slid down her pink blush colored cheeks. She'd put so much time and effort into planning the perfect birthday celebration for Jamil, but now he wasn't even answering her calls. As she stood crying, McKinley could not come to grips with the concept that Jamil could be that blatantly disrespectful.

At this point in their relationship they should've been beyond all of the petty nonsense. He should have known that his actions would affect her in a negative way. He should have known that her heart felt like it was being choked with his bare hands. He should have known that she wouldn't be able to sleep or eat until she heard the sound of his voice or the feel of his lips on her clit.

They'd been together three years. It was time out for all the bullshit, yet McKinley loved him too much to let him go. Wondering if she'd somehow missed his call; McKinley walked across the room and picked up her phone. The words *One Missed Call* were nowhere to be found on the display. Determined to get an explanation for his absence, McKinley called Jamil again, but he still wouldn't pick up the phone.

Mad as hell, McKinley decided to turn off her phone. She would show his ass. No way when he decided he wanted to be bothered with her would she make it easy for him to reach her. But as soon as she turned off her phone she wondered had she made the right decision. Determined not to second guess her decision, McKinley gathered her things and went inside her bedroom.

The entire room was stark white with accents of black and yellow. The covers on her platform bed were white and at the end of it she had a black-and-white African cloth. On both sides of her bed were mirrored nightstands. On top of the nightstands were white lamps and small vases filled with yellow roses.

Stripping down to nothing but her panties, McKinley placed on a white wifebeater and climbed into bed. She hoped that watching a little television would ease the sinking sensation in the pit of her stomach. Since it was a Friday night there wasn't much on TV except one of her favorite shows, E's *Fashion Police*. McKinley adored Joan Rivers and her sharp comedic timing.

Yes, the show was entertaining and even brought a smile to her face from time to time, but she couldn't help feeling like with each breath she took she was drowning. After McKinley watched *Fashion Police* and TLC's *Four Weddings* and *Say Yes to the Dress: Big Bliss,* she unknowingly drifted off to sleep. It was almost 4:00 when the sound of Jamil's heavy footsteps woke her up. McKinley opened her eyes slowly as Jamil climbed into bed and lay behind her.

"You woke?" he asked, wrapping his arm around her waist.

McKinley could smell the scent of liquor on his breath.

"I am now," she replied, dryly.

"You mad at me?" He kissed the back of her neck.

"What you think?" she spat sarcastically.

"My bad, man. I got caught up."

"Caught up doing what? You know I had plans for us to do something tonight." Jamil didn't answer.

"Uh hello?" she said, annoyed.

After still not getting a reply, McKinley looked over her shoulder and found Jamil with his head against the pillow asleep.

You have got to be fuckin' kiddin' me, she thought

"Wake yo' ass up!" She pushed his arm with brute force.

Jamil snapped his eyes opened. "I'm up! I'm up!"

"No, you're not. Yo' ass was asleep."

"No, I wasn't. I swear to God I'm up."

"What I say then?" McKinley quipped.

"Babe, I'm listening. Just give me a minute. I'm fucked up right now," Jamil said, looking like he was about to throw up.

"Get away from me." McKinley jerked her arm away.

"Stop!" Jamil demanded, pulling her back into him.

"No." McKinley elbowed him. "You get on my nerves with this shit. Where were you tonight?"

"No, the question is why the fuck you have yo' phone off?" Jamil countered.

"No way are you gon' try and flip this shit around on me," McKinley said, flabbergasted. "You played me tonight."

"I love how you try to act all innocent and shit." Jamil turned her over onto her back and lay on top of her. "Answer the fuckin' question. Why was your phone off?"

"'Cause I wanted it off, that's why," McKinley spat back, trying her best to hide how bad she wanted him.

Words couldn't describe how fine Jamil was. Just the sight of him turned her on. He and Chad Ochocinco could've been twins. Jamil's skin was the color of hot cocoa on a cold winter's day and he rocked a bald head like no other. His eyes were shaped like oval shaped diamonds and his full lips and goatee drew her in every time she looked at his face. His athletic build made her and every other woman on planet Earth's mouths water.

Jamil was a bad boy with a capital B. He owned and operated a construction company, but his main source of income came from selling heroin. McKinley knew that his occupation was dangerous and could one day put her in jeopardy, but to be his girl was the risk she was willing to take.

"What, you had some nigga over here or something?" He mean mugged her.

"Please." McKinley rolled her eyes.

"Don't make me fuck you up, McKinley," Jamil warned.

"Whatever," she huffed.

"You can stop with the tough girl act now. I said I was sorry." Jamil kissed her lightly on the mouth.

"Just go 'head, Jamil." McKinley pushed him back.

"You don't mean that." He kissed her again more forcefully.

"Yes, I do. You gon' stop doing me like this," she protested with her mouth while spreading her legs wider.

"I said I was sorry." Jamil tenderly kissed her neck.

"No, you're not." McKinley closed her eyes.

Jamil's tongue was wreaking havoc on her neck.

"You know I love you," he whispered, pushing her tank top up.

McKinley's skin smelled like cotton candy. He had to taste her. Her exposed breasts aroused him. Jamil planted soft kisses all over McKinley's collarbone and chest until his lips met her hardened nipples.

"You forgive me?" he asked, making her melt.

McKinley clutched her pelvis tight and released a soft moan. She loved it when Jamil's wet tongue flickered across her nipples. It was the one thing that made her instantly wet. Jamil took both of her supple breasts into his hands and pressed them together. The sight reminded him of two water balloons.

Then he took his tongue and ran it back and forth across each of her breasts until she couldn't take it anymore. Realizing he had her right where he wanted her, Jamil proceeded further down. McKinley watched in sheer delight, wondering what his next move would be. Yes, she could've put up a better fight, but having sex with Jamil was her kryptonite and he used it against her every time.

His dick game constantly had her in a tailspin. Every day that passed, she yearned for it more and more. Gripping her thick thighs, Jamil pushed them both back. McKinley's knees almost touched her chest. McKinley knew she was in big trouble. When Jamil went low he'd stay there for hours.

"You still don't forgive me?" He gazed up at her with lust in his eyes.

"Uh ah." McKinley shook her head, giving him a sly grin.

"Okay." Jamil nodded.

Then without warning, he dove headfirst into the lips of her pussy. There wasn't any slow build up. Jamil went at is as if it was the very last time he'd get to taste her.

"Oh, my God," McKinley moaned, arching her head back.

All she could feel was Jamil's tongue running feverishly over her pussy.

"You forgive me?" Jamil asked, never once stopping.

"Nooooooo." McKinley clutched the sheets.

Without showing any mercy Jamil took his fingers and opened up the lips of her pussy. McKinley's pretty pink clit was only inches away from his wet tongue. But before he gave her another oral education, Jamil massaged her pussy with his hand. Then he took two of his fingers and dipped them deep into her honey pot. McKinley was dizzy. The in-and-out motion of his fingers, plus the sensation of his tongue circling around her clit was spellbinding.

"You still don't forgive me?" Jamil questioned, sucking anxiously on her clit.

"Nooooooo." McKinley's legs began to shake.

Fed up with playing games, Jamil got up on his knees and unzipped his jeans. Lying on top of her, he kissed her mouth passionately. As their tongues swirled around each other Jamil stuck the tip of his dick into McKinley's pussy. The sheer force and girth of his manhood caused her eyes to fly open.

"You forgive me now, don't you?" Jamil grinded his dick in a circular motion.

"Yes, I forgive you, Daddy. I forgive you."

*Lately I've been feelin'
like you're taking me for
granted."*

*Brandy
"Apart"*

High from the night before, McKinley put the finishing touches on the breakfast she'd prepared for Jamil—French toast, two hard fried eggs, ham, Jimmy Dean sausage links, grits, sliced strawberries and a cup of freshly squeezed orange juice. With everything hot and ready to go, McKinley placed his plate on a wooden serving tray and headed back to her bedroom.

"Babe," she called out to him.

"Babe." She nudged him with her knee, causing him to steer in his sleep. "Babe."

"Huh?" Jamil groaned.

"Wake up." McKinley nudged him once more.

This time Jamil opened his eyes.

"What's up?" He turned over.

"I made breakfast." McKinley smiled gleefully.

"Word?" He squinted his eyes and sat up.
"Yeah." She handed him a napkin. "Oh, and since I wasn't able to give you your gift last night, here." McKinley handed him a gift box that fit into the palm of his hand.

Jamil ripped off the gift wrap, opened the box and found a Frank Muller watch with the words, *With you time stands still,* engraved on the inside of the band.

"Thanks, babe." He leaned forward and gave McKinley a quick peck on the lips.

"You really like it?" she asked, hopeful.

"Yeah." Jamil closed the box and placed it beside him on the bed.

McKinley watched him silently. It seemed to her that he was more into the breakfast than he was the gift she'd spent weeks getting customized.

"You got some more syrup?" Jamil asked, stuffing his mouth with sausage.

"Yeah, there's some in the kitchen. You want me to get you some more?" McKinley asked, trying to hide her discontent.

"Would you please?" Jamil took a gulp of orange juice from his cup.

McKinley got up and walked to the kitchen, wondering could he see the sadness that was so clearly written all over her face.

"Ay, what time is it?" Jamil yelled.

"Nine-thirty," McKinley said with the syrup in her hand.

"Oh shit. I gotta go." Jamil removed the tray from his lap and began put on his jeans.

"Where you going? You haven't even finished your food yet," McKinley said, feeling her temperature rise.

"I got something I need to take care of." Jamil zipped up his jeans.

"Like, you're fuckin' wit' me right?" McKinley folded her arms across her chest.

"No." Jamil pulled his shirt on over his head.

"Okay, it's bad enough you played me last night. Now you're gettin' ready to play me again?"

"It's too early in the morning, McKinley. Don't start that shit."

Jamil placed on the watch he wore last night.

"What shit?" McKinley scrunched up her face.

"All that fuckin' complaining. Let me go take care of this and I'll get up wit you later." Jamil kissed her on the cheek.

McKinley stood motionless. She wanted to say more, but it was useless. Jamil was already out the door. Fuming, she walked over to the bed and picked up the tray of food when she noticed his gift sitting on the bed. *Inconsiderate bastard*, she hissed inwardly, stomping toward the kitchen. McKinley was so mad that she emptied the entire tray of food, including the dishes, in the trash.

She really didn't know how much more of Jamil's insensitive attitude she could take. The shit was getting old and fast. She deserved to be treated like a queen. Yes, Jamil provided her with a lavish lifestyle that she wouldn't be able to maintain without his assistance. But all of the money in the world couldn't buy happiness and peace of mind. McKinley ran her hand through her long black hair as her house phone began to ring. Hoping that it was Jamil calling to say that he was sorry, she raced over to the phone.

To her dismay, it was her mother. McKinley rolled her eyes and let out a breath of air. She really wasn't in the mood to talk to her. Every time they talked their conversation somehow steered into how foolish she was for dropping her life back in St. Louis to be with a man whom she barely knew and who wasn't, in her mother's words, worth shit.

But what her mother didn't and couldn't understand was that from the moment they met, McKinley fell head over heels in love. She'd met Jamil while on vacation in Miami with her girlfriends. After spending every waking moment together, when it was time for her to leave the two couldn't bear to part. They'd had a whirlwind romance that neither wanted to end.

Everyone, including her mother and friends, told her she was crazy for jumping into a relationship with a man she barely knew and for giving up her job as an underwriter to stay in a city where she knew no one. But McKinley didn't care. She was a sucker for love at first sight, so when Jamil promised her the world she believed him. Deciding she'd talk to her mother later, McKinley let her voicemail pick up the call. Just as she was about to go back to her bedroom and sulk, the phone rang again.

"C'mon, Ma. What is it?" McKinley whined, looking at the caller ID. But it wasn't her mother calling; it was her BFF of three years, Kristen, who lived two floors down.

After moving into the building, McKinley and Kristen became instant friends. They both had a shared love for designer frocks, reality television and good food. Plus, Kristen's boyfriend and Jamil ran in the same circle, so Kristen understood the trials and tribulations of dating a man who was not only wealthy, but full of drama.

"Hello?" McKinley answered the phone.

"Whaaaaat? I can't believe yo' ass up this time of the morning."

"Shut up." McKinley chuckled, sitting down on the couch.

"I just saw your nigga leave as I was coming in."

"It's only nine-fifteen, Kristen. Where in the hell have you been already?"

"While yo' ass was in the bed, fuckin' and suckin', I went to the gym and then to the grocery store. Something you know nothin' about," Kristen said with a laugh.

"You got that right," McKinley responded unenthusiastically.

"What's wrong wit you?" Kristen asked, hearing the sound of sadness in her voice.

"Nothin'." McKinley sighed.

"McKinley, this is me. I know when there's something wrong wit' you. What has Jamil done now?"

"Girl, he just gets on my nerve." McKinley rolled her eyes. "You know I planned that whole big ta da for his birthday, and do you know he didn't even bother to show up? I sat in that restaurant for damn near an hour and a half like a goddamn dummy before I finally said fuck it and went home."

"So what was his excuse for not showing up?" Kristen asked, unlocking the door to her apartment.

"Now that I think about it, he never really gave me an explanation," McKinley replied, having what Oprah Winfrey called an "aha moment."

"Now that I think about it, instead of him tellin' me where he was, that muthafucka turned the shit around on me and went off on me for turning my phone off."

"Tricky bastard." Kristen grinned.

"I can't believe that nigga got over on me again," McKinley replied in disbelief.

"Niggas," Kristen said, putting up her groceries. "Can't live with 'em, can't live without 'em."

"I'm just tired of him treating me like this. He's just so fuckin' insensitive."

"Aren't all men?" Kristen joked.

"I guess you have a point," McKinley agreed.

"Look, girl," Kristen stopped dead in her tracks. "Fuck Jamil. If he wanna act a fool let him. Tony ass on some bullshit, too, but you think I'm over here on suicide watch? No. I'm doin' me 'cause guess what? Ain't none of this shit new. We know how these niggas are and we're both choosing to stay, so why continue to cry and whine every time they do something fucked up? You think they trippin' off us right now? No. So let's take a page from their book and not trip off they ass either."

"You're right." McKinley let out a much-needed breath.

She wanted to be strong like Kristen, but deep down inside she knew thoughts of Jamil would control her mind for the rest of the day. The shit was sickening. It was like she lived and breathed him.

"Check it. How about we have a 'I'm Doin' Me Day'? We're gonna get dressed, get our nails and feet done, grab lunch, then go shoppin'. And to finish out our 'I'm Doin' Me Day' we'll put on our flyest outfits and head to Mansion tonight. What do you say?" Kristen exclaimed. "And I'm not takin' no for an answer," she added.

"Well, I guess that's a yes then." McKinley laughed.

"Oh, and if Tony or Jamil call we have to promise not to pick up the phone."

"Now you reaching," McKinley countered.

"Quit being a punk. Besides, how many times have you called Jamil and he didn't answer your calls? Case in point, last night on his birthday. One day of giving that nigga yo' ass to kiss won't hurt. If anything, it'll put a fire under his ass and make him act right for a change. And another thing—"

McKinley caved in. "Okay, okay, okay. I swear, you should've went to law school 'cause yo' ass can talk a muthafucka into anything."

"I'll take that as a compliment," Kristen replied. "Now be ready by eleven."

"A'ight."

"And don't take all day, McKinley. You got almost two hours to get ready," Kristen stressed.

"Okay, heffa."

"Whatever, bitch, meet me in the lobby at eleven," Kristen said before hanging up.

"Deuces."

XoXo

"I swear yo' ass gon' be late for your own funeral," Kristen said, pulling out the parking lot of her and McKinley's building.

"You can't rush perfection." McKinley looked in the rearview mirror and applied another coat of pink Chanel lip gloss.

"Bitch, you look a'ight." Kristen pushed the passenger's visor mirror up in its appropriate position, snapping it closed.

"Uh." McKinley screwed up her face. "Don't be a hater."

"Chile, please. I'm far from a hater. I mean, have you taken a good look at me lately? I'm the shit, bitch."

"Whatever. You look a'ight, but please believe you ain't flyer then me." McKinley grinned as the wind whipped through their hair.

McKinley would never admit it to Kristen, because she was so vain, but Kristen was supermodel gorgeous. She was tall and statuesque with a sepia skin tone. Kristen rocked her hair in a super cute bob with blunt bangs. Kristen had a full bust and plump ass to fill out her clothes.

"So where are we going?" McKinley inquired. "'Cause it's like ninety-five degrees outside and I'm not tryin' to be out in the heat. 'Cause you know with the kinda hair I got my shit gon' be lookin' like Chaka Khan's in a matter of seconds. And I did not spend a half an hour flat ironing my hair for nothin'.'"

"Now I see why Jamil stood you up, 'cause you's one complaining bitch." Kristen grimaced.

"Just answer the question, trick," McKinley snapped.

"We're going to Blush to get our mani-pedis, lil' nosy-ass girl."

"Cool, 'cause I wanna change my color." McKinley looked down at her nails as her cell phone started to ring. "Uh ah," McKinley snarled.

"What?" Kristen looked over.

"Jamil's callin' me."

"You bet' not answer that phone," Kristen warned.

"I'm not." McKinley slid her phone back inside her purse. "Like you said, I'm doin' me today." She smiled brightly.

"She put up wit it 'cause she know that dick be dynamite."

Masspike Miles featuring Rick Ross
"Nasty"

After being fully pampered and shopping until her wallet screamed "STOOOOOOOOOOOOP," McKinley returned home. She couldn't wait to dump her things out on the bed and get dolled up for a night on the town with her girl. Kristen had been right. Their day of doin' them was empowering. It felt good not to sit in the house and sulk over Jamil's latest disappointment.

He'd been blowin' up her cell phone non-stop, but McKinley never once caved in and answered the phone. It felt good to have him wondering where she was and what she was doing. McKinley dug inside her Birken bag and pulled out her key to unlock the door. As soon as she stepped across the threshold, she dropped her bags and screamed.

"Where the fuck you been?" Jamil barked, sitting on the couch.

"Boy, you scared the shit outta me." McKinley held her chest.

"Fuck all of that. Answer the question. Where you been?"

"Out. Why?" McKinley curled her upper lip and bent over to pick up her bags.

"You know why. Why the fuck you ain't been answering my calls?"

"The same reason you didn't answer mine last night," McKinley shot back sarcastically.

"Oh, now you on some ole other shit. Why everything gotta be a game wit' you? I'm gettin' real sick of you not answering my calls 'cause you call yo'self being mad. How about I get that muthafucka turned off then, since you don't like answering it. Then we can just go our separate ways. You can take yo' ass back to Saint Louis. 'Cause you ain't about to play me like I'm some bitch-ass nigga," Jamil barked.

"Really, Jamil?" McKinley cocked her head to the side, outdone by his statement. "Don't you think you're carrying on a bit?"

"No."

"Well, why is it every time I do something you don't like you wanna call it quits?"

"Look, this is my life. Anything could've happened to me and you wouldn't have known. All because you wanna play tit for tat."

McKinley hated to admit it, but Jamil had a point.

"You know what? You're right. I just feel like sometimes you don't care," she admitted.

"If I didn't care I wouldn't be here. Look," he waved his hand. "I'm tired of talkin'. Come here." He beckoned for her to sit on his lap.

McKinley sauntered over to Jamil, trying her best not to smile.

"I love you." He stared deep into her eyes. "Don't shit else matter."

"I know it's just that—"

"Shhhhhhh." Jamil cut her off by placing his index finger up to her lips. "I don't wanna talk no more. I wanna see what you got on underneath this lil bitty ass dress." He slid his hands underneath her skirt and massaged her bare ass.

"Aww, yeah?" He smiled, surprised. "Yo' ass really in trouble now. Give me a kiss," Jamil demanded.

McKinley placed her hands on the side of his face and slowly kissed his lips.

"You gon' give me some?"
McKinley quickly got up. "Uh ah, Jamil, we are not gettin' ready to have sex. I promised Kristen I'd go out wit' her tonight." She got up.

He looked up at her. "So going out wit' yo' homegirl is more important than spending time wit' ya' man?"

"Here you go." McKinley groaned, tucking her hair behind her ear.

Jamil nodded his head repeatedly then unzipped his jeans. "It's cool."

He pulled out his dick and began talking to it. "You see how she doing us, man?" *This nigga is not fighting fair,* McKinley thought, licking her lips.

If there was one thing in life she couldn't resist, it was an end-of-the-season sale and Jamil's big, brown juicy dick. To her, it was a work of art and to see it sticking straight up in the air like a missile, while Jamil ran his hand up and down its shaft, put her in a trance. McKinley didn't even realize that she'd taken him in her mouth until she was on her knees. She thoroughly enjoyed sucking Jamil's dick. It always seemed to glide in and out of her mouth with velvet ease.

"Fuck," Jamil groaned.

McKinley sucked his dick like a porn star. Wanting a better view, Jamil combed McKinley's hair over to the side with his fingertips and watched with pleasure as she slid her tongue from his balls up to the tip of his dick. Ready to put his thing down, Jamil said, "Come here."

McKinley straddled him and eased down slowly onto his dick.

"Damn, baby, you wet." Jamil gripped her butt cheeks and helped her bounce up and down.

"I know, baby, this dick feels so good." She whimpered as her cell phone rang.

"Mmm, hold up. Let me get that, that's Kristen." She tried reaching for her phone.

"You wasn't answering yo' phone earlier, so don't answer it now. I got this. You concentrate on riding this dick." Jamil slapped her on the ass and answered her phone.

"Are you ready?" Kristen asked, dryly.

"Yo, listen. She ain't comin'. I mean, well, she is cumming, but you get the picture." Jamil chuckled.

"Jamil," McKinley shrieked, still bouncing.

"Oh, my God! Y'all are disgusting. Bye!" Kristen hung up.

Jamil cracked a smile and hung up, too.

"You love this dick, don't you?" He slapped her ass again.

"Oooooh, yes," McKinley screamed, feeling an orgasm coming near.

"Shit, babe." She rocked back and forth. "Oh, my God, this dick feels so good!"

"You finna come?" Jamil could feel a nut build in the tip of his dick.

"Yes!"

"Me, too." Jamil came without pulling out.

Calming down from her orgasmic high, McKinley stood up and plopped down onto the couch.

"That was so good, I wanna buy you a short set." She panted heavily, trying to catch her breath.

"You want something to drink?" Jamil asked, going inside the kitchen.

"Yeah, get me a bottled water, please."

Jamil quickly returned with both of their drinks.

"Thanks, baby." McKinley took a long gulp. "Whew! I needed that."

"Why don't you go get dressed, so we can go out?" Jamil asked.

"For real?" McKinley looked at him surprised.

"Yeah."

"Bet." She jumped up from the couch and raced to her bedroom.

XoXo

It was midnight when McKinley and Jamil walked hand in hand into club Mansion. Mansion was one of the premiere places to be in Miami. On any given night, you could run into a top-line celebrity like Kourtney Kardashian, Diddy or Drake. There was always a party being thrown by an A-list celeb or a one-time-only performance by your favorite artist. Being inside Mansion was like being transported into another realm. The space was humongous. More than five hundred people could fit into the club.

But even with the slew of scantily clad women in the crowd

PRIMA DONNA

none could outshine McKinley. Homegirl was fresh to death
in a colorful, multi-strand, beaded necklace, white scoop-neck
oversized T-shirt with the sleeves rolled up, lime-green bandage
skirt and purple Manolo Blahnik, patent leather heels. Her long
hair was parted down the center and flat ironed bone straight. To
finish off the look she rocked a hot pink, Valentino Noeud d'Amore
clutch. Jamil didn't look too bad either.

He donned a blue jean jacket with the sleeves shrugged up.
In the pocket of the jacket was a crème colored handkerchief.
Underneath the jacket, he wore a blue V-neck tee. To complete
his look, he sported a pair of dirty wash jeans and brown leather
combat boots. McKinley and Jamil were such a stunning couple
that partygoers couldn't help but stop and stare as they walked
by. As McKinley strutted up the steps to the VIP area, she spotted
Kristen on the dance floor, dancing as if she didn't have a care in
the world.

"Hold up, babe. I see Kristen. Let me go say hi to her,"
McKinley said in mid-stride.

"A'ight. Tell her to come up in VIP wit' us," Jamil suggested.

"Okay," McKinley said, turning around.

The crowd on the dance floor was so thick that it took
McKinley almost five minutes to get to Kristen. Sleigh Bells
"Infinity Guitar" was blasting through the speakers and Kristen
was all into the beat.

"You look cute," McKinley yelled into her ear over the loud
music.

Kristen spun around.

"Bitch!" She opened her arms wide and hugged McKinley.
"What are you doing here? I thought you were standing me up for

Page 31

yo' nigga?"

"I technically did. He's upstairs in VIP. You mad at me?" McKinley poked out her bottom lip.

"You fake, but whatever." Kristen waved her off.

"C'mon, you wanna come upstairs wit' us?"

"What, so I can be the third wheel?" Kristen cocked her head back. "I think not."

"Girl, you know it ain't nothin' like that. C'mon." McKinley took her hand, not taking no for an answer.

To both McKinley and Kristen's surprise, when they entered the VIP area they found Jamil and Kristen's boyfriend, Tony, smoking cigars and poppin' bottles with one another.

"Did you know he was here?" Kristen asked McKinley.

"No. I'm just as surprised as you are," McKinley responded.

Kristen stomped over to Tony. "What the hell are you doing here?"

"I knew you was gon' have yo' hot ass up in the club tonight, so I decided to pop up on you. You still mad at me?" Tony invaded Kristen's personal space.

"What you think?" Kristen replied, not backing down.

"I take that as a yes." He laughed.

"You damn right." Kristen rolled her eyes.

"Why you so damn mean? You know that shit turn me on." Tony wrapped her up in his arms.

"I can't stand you." Kristen shook her head and cracked a smile.

Happy to see her friend smiling, McKinley walked over to her man who was holding her a glass of champagne.

Jamil held up his glass. "To us."

"To us." McKinley tapped her glass against his then took a sip when "Wet" by Snoop Dogg came on.

"Aww shit! That's my song." She sat her glass down and started grooving.

Kristen loved the song, too, and started jamming to the song with her.

"Tell me, baby, are you wet? I just wanna get you wet." They sang the song while rolling their hips.

Jamil loved nothing more than to see McKinley lose herself within the beat of a song. McKinley could dance her ass off. Her moves were so sensual and hypnotizing. She knew how to roll her stomach and hips just like a belly dancer and pop her ass like a video vixen. Jamil watched as her round booty twirled around in circles. The skintight skirt she wore emphasized her moves and curves. The sight was too much for him to handle. It made him dizzy with lust.

McKinley looked over her shoulder at him. She could see the look of desire in his eyes. Knowing just how to turn him on, she backed her ass up on him. Jamil placed his hands on her hips and danced with her. For the rest of the night the two love birds enjoyed each other's company. They laughed, drank and danced until the wee hours of the morning.

"I'm pissed off. I want you to feel the same."

Dawn Richards
"I'm Just Sayin'"

After a long fun-filled night of grooving to their favorite Hip Hop and R&B artists and sipping on the finest liquor Mansion had to offer, McKinley and Jamil returned home. As soon as they walked through the door, Jamil stripped down and went to bed. Normally, McKinley would've gone right to bed, too, but she had to clean her kitchen. The dishes from the previous morning were still in the sink and McKinley was not raised to go to bed with a dirty kitchen.

While Jamil lay underneath the covers, soaking up the central air, she stood barefoot at the kitchen sink, washing the dishes by hand. McKinley was halfway done when she heard a loud buzzing sound. Wondering where the sound was coming from, McKinley turned off the faucet and listened closely. The buzzing noise wasn't coming from the kitchen so she walked into the living room. McKinley was so focused on locating the noise that she didn't notice Jamil's Lanvin sneakers and jeans in the middle of the floor, causing her to almost trip and fall.

"I'ma kick his ass," she hissed, bending over to pick up his things.

Then she heard the buzzing sound come from his jeans.

Who in the hell is callin' him this early in the morning, she thought, holding his jeans up to her chest. Immediately, memories of Jamil's past infidelities came rushing to her mind. Yeah, she'd forgiven him for his past transgressions, but once he'd cheated on her that feeling of betrayal never went away. She knew it was wrong to snoop because when you look for trouble you usually find it, but she had to know who was calling him. Quietly, she reached into his pocket and pulled out his cell phone. The screen revealed that he had a text message from someone named T. The message read:

From: T
Where r u? I'm @ home.

Sent:
Sun, May 21, 4:37 am

Chill bumps immediately spread across McKinley's arms and legs she was so enraged. Breathing heavily, she glanced over her shoulder to ensure the coast was clear, it was. She had to confirm that this T person was a girl, so McKinley pressed the call button and dialed the person's phone. Two rings later, a woman answered the phone. Hearing the woman's voice crushed her heart. Tears instantly formed in her eyes, but she was determined not to cry.

"Hello?" the woman said again.

McKinley didn't bother to say anything. Instead, she ended the call and went back into the kitchen. Grabbing a pin and a piece of paper, she quickly jotted down the girl's number and stashed it in one of the kitchen drawers she knew Jamil never went in. Now that she had all the ammunition she needed to pounce on his cheating ass, McKinley raced up the stairs and barged into their bedroom.

"Jamil!" she yelled, pushing his arm.

"What?" He screwed up his face.

"Wake up!" McKinley spat.

"What the fuck are you yellin' for?" Jamil turned over onto his side.

"Get yo' ass up!" McKinley yelled even louder.

"Yo, on the real, McKinley. I ain't in the mood for no bullshit tonight," Jamil warned. "It's four-thirty in the morning. What the fuck do you want?" he groaned.

"Who the fuck is T?" McKinley held up his phone.

"What?" He eyed her, confused.

"Please." McKinley put her hand up as if to say pause. "Let's not play dumb. Just answer the fuckin' question. Who is T?"

"I don't know." He looked away.

"Really? Well, apparently she knows you 'cause she just sent you a text message, asking where you were at?" McKinley threw his phone at him, almost hitting him in the head with it.

"You out yo' fuckin' mind?" Jamil dodged the throw and sat up. "Don't throw shit else at me, McKinley. 'Cause if I get to throwin' shit you ain't gon' like it. And what the fuck you doing going through my phone?"

"Just answer the fuckin' question! Who is T?" McKinley shot sternly.
"A girl," Jamil replied sarcastically.

"I know she's a girl, douche bag. Who is she?"

"Since you're so fuckin' nosy. She's one of my business pot'nahs."
"Do I look that stupid to you?" McKinley placed her hand on her hip.

"Honestly, you do 'cause you always jumpin' to conclusions, assuming shit and you don't know what the hell you're talkin' about."

"What kind of business partner calls you at four o'clock in the morning? Just admit it, Jamil. You're cheating on me again, aren't you?"

"I ain't gotta put up with this shit." He flung his legs out of the bed and got up.

"Where you think you going?" She eyed him in disbelief.

"Where it look like I'm going? Home!" He shot over his shoulder.

"Really, Jamil? So you just gon' leave? You not gon' even tell me the truth?" McKinley followed him down the stairs.

"I have told you the truth. It's up to you to believe it. And where the fuck are my clothes?" He searched the first floor.

"In the kitchen." McKinley folded her arms across her chest.

"Why are my clothes in the kitchen?" Jamil barked.

"'Cause I took'em in there. That's why."

"So you just going through all of my shit, huh." Jamil smirked, placing on his jeans.

"Whatever," McKinley rolled her eyes. "I don't see shit funny."

"Yous a fuckin' trip, you know that? You invade my privacy and got the nerve to have an attitude?"

"You damn right, I got an attitude. You got bitches callin' yo' phone and then gon' sit up here and lie to my face about it. Are you crazy?"

"You can believe what you wanna believe. I ain't gotta explain myself to you." Jamil took his car keys from out of his pocket.

"So you seriously gettin' ready to leave?" McKinley said, distraught.

She couldn't believe that he wouldn't own up to the fact that he'd been caught. Instead, like always, he flipped the situation around and made her feel like the guilty party.

"Yeah, I am," he confirmed. "Until you can learn how to trust me, I don't think we need to be wit' each other."

"So not only are you leaving, but you're breaking up with me?" McKinley said stunned.

"I mean, what else you want me to do? You don't trust me."

"And you've given me every reason under the sun not to. All you do is lie."

"Whatever, man. I'll holla at you later." Jamil placed his hand on the knob.

"Are you serious right now?" McKinley began to cry.

She didn't understand how he could be upset when he was the one who'd done wrong.

"I'll call you tomorrow or something." He opened the door and left.

McKinley thought about running after him, but running after him would only make her feel stupid in the end. When Jamil was on his soapbox he wouldn't come down until he had McKinley down on her knees or until he had no other choice but to confess. It was sad, but that was how he was. McKinley just had to figure out what her next move would be. She couldn't let another day go by without knowing where she really stood with Jamil.

XoXo

McKinley knocked on Kristen's door the following morning. "Code 10! Code 10! We got a man-down situation."

"What the hell is going on?" Kristen opened up the door and let McKinley in.

"I'm sorry, were you asleep?" McKinley asked, noticing she had on a robe.

"No, just gettin' my bed rocked," Kristen said out of the side of her mouth.

"Oh, my bad, is Tony here?" McKinley whispered back.

"Yeah, I am." He came out of the back, pulling his T-shirt on over his head.

"You gettin' ready to leave?" Kristen asked disappointed.

"Yeah, I'ma shake, but I'll be back in a couple of hours." He kissed her on the forehead. "I love you."

"I love you, too." Kristen poked out her bottom lip.

"Bye, Tony." McKinley waved.

"Stay up, McKinley." He walked out of the door.

"Now what the hell is the emergency, cockblocker?" Kristen tightened her robe.

"You will not believe what happened last night." McKinley barged into Kristen's kitchen and started rummaging through her cabinets. "You got any saltines? I need something to settle my stomach." McKinley looked over her shoulder.

"Yeah, in the cabinet on your left and please tell me you're not pregnant." Kristen followed her into the kitchen.

"Hell no. I've been up drinkin' and thinkin'."

"Why?" Kristen sat on top of the counter.

"Some girl named T texted Jamil last night when we got home

from the club."

"Get outta here." Kristen crossed her legs.

"Yes, and when I confronted him about it he gon' lie and say she one of his 'business pot'nahs'." McKinley made air quotes with her fingers. "Then he got an attitude wit' me."

"Ain't that what they always do?" Kristen chuckled.

"I know he lying though."

"Uh, duh." Kristen rolled her neck. "Yeah, that nigga lyin'. You think he just gon' come out and say, yeah I'm stickin' my dick in her."

"Well, we gettin' ready to find out for sure." McKinley went into her back pocket and pulled out a piece of paper. "'Cause you gettin' ready to call her."
"You say what now?" Kristen cocked her head back.

"Please, Kristen." McKinley clasped her hands together. "I'm too emotional to talk to her, and plus, I might cuss her out if she say step outta line."

"And what the hell you think I'ma do?"

"C'mon, Kristen. I would do it for you. Hell, I *have* done it for you."

"Give me the goddamn number." Kristen snatched the piece of paper from McKinley's hand.

"Thank you," McKinley smiled.

Kristen grabbed the cordless phone and dialed the girl's number, but not before pressing *67, and putting the call on speakerphone.

"Hello?"

"Hi, may I speak to T?" Kristen asked sweetly.

"Who is this?" the woman asked.

"This is McKinley, Jamil's girlfriend."

"Uh, huh?" the girl said unfazed.

"Is this T?" Kristen asked again.

"Yeah, this me," T answered with an attitude.
"Listen, I'm not callin' you to argue or anything like that. I just
wanted to know if you and Jamil messing around."

McKinley crossed her fingers and prayed to God that the girl's
answer would be no.

"I think you need to ask Jamil that," T remarked dryly.
"So I take that as a yes," Kristen responded.

"Like I said, you need to ask your man that question," T replied
before hanging up.

"Bitch," Kristen spat, hanging up as well. "Well, I guess you
got your answer." She gave McKinley a sad face.

Heartbroken, McKinley placed down the saltines and stood
paralyzed. She felt so stupid for even giving Jamil the benefit of
the doubt. He didn't deserve it, just like he didn't deserve her.

"So what are you going to do?" Kristen asked.

"I'ma fuck his ass up. That's what I'ma do." McKinley pulled
out her cell phone and called him.

"What's up?" Jamil answered the phone with a smile.

He just knew that McKinley was calling him to apologize.

"Come get your shit," McKinley hissed.

"What?" Jamil said, caught off guard.

"You heard me. Come get your shit. I am done fuckin' wit' you. You've been cheating on me this whole time with that bitch." "You still on that? I told you I wasn't doing nothin'," Jamil replied mildly.

"Just stop lying. I talked to the girl, Jamil."

"You did what?" His voice went up an octave.

"Yeah, that's right. I talked to her and she told me everything that I needed to know, so come get your shit 'cause I'm done." McKinley pressed the *End* button.

As soon as she hung up Jamil called her right back, but she didn't even bother to pick up.

"You gon' be okay, friend?" Kristen asked concerned.

"I will be once I get his ass out of my life. Look, let me go back up to my apartment. I'm sure he's on his way over there."

"Okay." Kristen hopped down from the counter. "Call me if you need me."

"I will." McKinley left out and boarded the elevator.

By the time she reached her apartment Jamil had called her over ten times. On a mission to rid herself of him, McKinley stormed into her place and began collecting all of his things. She'd successfully thrown his underwear and socks and half of his clothes down the stairs when he came walking through the door.

"McKinley," he called out for her.

"I don't wanna hear shit you got to say, Jamil. Just get your shit and go." She threw one of his coats over the rail.

"Have you lost yo' mind? Stop throwing my shit," he yelled from the first floor.
"Fuck you," McKinley shouted back.

"Yo, will you let me explain?" He dodged a boot that was being thrown at his head then ran up the steps.

"Explain what? That you're a fuckin' lyin' ass piece of shit? I can't believe you've been cheating on me again. Here I was thinkin' we were doing better, but no, you don't give a fuck about me. You gon' continue to do you."

"I'm tellin' you I didn't cheat on you." Jamil got into her face and held her by the arms.

"Let me go, Jamil." McKinley closed her eyes.
"No. Not until you listen to me."
"I don't wanna hear shit you got to say. All I wanna see is your back walking out the door, straight up."

"So you not gon' let me tell you what happened?"

"What about "I'm done fuckin' wit you" don't you understand? It's over. Just get your shit and go."

"That's really how you feel?" Jamil said, taken aback by her persistence.

"Yeah."
"Well, fuck you then." He let her go.
"Fuck me?" McKinley's eyes grew wide. "Fuck me?" Her lips trembled.

"Nigga, fuck you," she spat as he walked down the steps and out the door.

XoXo

Around ten o'clock that night McKinley sat in bed watching the Showtime hit *Shameless*. She had a bowl of buttered popcorn and a Mountain Dew slush to wash it down. She'd fully made it up in her mind that she and Jamil were done for good. She'd had enough of being tortured by his lies. It was time for her to take a cue from Kristen and the singer Fantasia and start doing her.

If she was going to be miserable then she'd much rather be miserable by herself. Laughing, she reached inside the bowl and pulled out a handful of popcorn when she received a text message from Jamil. McKinley rolled her eyes and viewed it.

From: Jamil
I'm sorry
Sent:
Fri, May 22, 10:22 pm

"You're sorry all right." She erased the message and threw her phone down.

A few minutes later he sent her another message.

From: Jamil
Baby, please 4give me. You know I can't live without u.
Sent:
Sun, May 22, 10:26 pm

"He is so wack." She smirked when he texted her again.

From: Jamil

C'mon, ma, don't do this. U know ur my baby. I luv u
Sent:
Sun, May 22, 10:28 pm
McKinley erased the message and continued to ignore him when he sent another message.

From: Jamil
Can I please come talk 2 u?
Sent:
Sun, May 22, 10:31 pm

McKinley inhaled deeply. She couldn't front, she liked to see Jamil beg. It made her feel like she was the one in charge. Plus, she'd wanted to hear from him anyway. It would've killed her if he hadn't tried reaching out to her, so she texted him back and said:

To: Jamil
Yeah
Sent:
Sun, May 22, 10:39 pm

A minute hadn't even gone by before she heard him enter the house.

"This muthafucka been standing outside this whole time," she said out loud to herself.

Jamil came up the stairs and stood in the doorway of their bedroom with his hands inside his pockets and stared at her.

He spoke softly. "What's up?"

"You tell me." McKinley cocked her head to the side.

"You know I love you like a fat kid love cake," he joked,

making her laugh.

"Whatever, Jamil."

"Real talk, you and I are good together; you know that, don't you?"

"Yeah, I know it." She placed her head down.

"You love me?"

"No." She bit the inside of her bottom lip.

"You know I can always tell when you're lying 'cause you bite the inside of your lip." Jamil came toward her and kissed her on the lips.

"Shut up." McKinley pushed him away.

"You gotta believe me, baby. I ain't fuckin' wit' nobody, but you."

"Well, why would she tell me to ask you if y'all mess around then?"

"I don't know. All I know is that I love you." Jamil took her into his arms.

"Jamil, I can't take too much more of this." McKinley's voice shook slightly.

"I know, baby, I know."

"No more tryin', tired of feelin' like I'm the only one dyin'."

Dawn Richards
"I'm Just Sayin'"

After a couple of blissful weeks together, McKinley awoke, expecting to see Jamil's face, but instead found that she was alone.

"I know that muthafucka didn't leave without sayin' nothin'." She snatched the covers from off of her and got up.

Dressed in one of Jamil's oversized T-shirts she searched the second floor of her apartment until she found him in the spare bedroom that she'd converted into an office/sitting room. There he was sitting on the couch with his feet propped up on a footstool, playing Call of Duty.

"I was gettin' ready to say." McKinley let out a sigh of relief.

He quickly looked up at her. "Say what?"

"Nothin'." McKinley went and sat on the arm of the couch. "How long have you been up?"

"Umm . . . almost two hours." Jamil focused in on the game.

"Why didn't you wake me?"

"'Cause I knew you were tired." He pressed the *A* button on the controller repeatedly.

"So you've been up almost two hours and the only thing you've accomplished is playing this dumb video game? Like really, Jamil? You couldn't have found something more productive to do with your time?"

"You complain entirely too much. If complaining was against the law you'd go to jail," he joked.

"Excuse you. I am not a complainer."

"Yeah, you are. How about instead of running your mouth all the time, you open up your eyes and take a look around before you get to judging."

"What have you done?" McKinley's face lit up with a smile.

"Go and see," Jamil said, putting the game on pause.

Before he knew it, McKinley was gone. If there was one thing on earth that McKinley loved more than she loved Chanel was a good surprise. McKinley raced down the steps and found that the dining room table had been completely set and was filled with every delectable breakfast food you could imagine.

"Oh, my God," she gushed, inching toward the table.

Jamil had outdone himself. There were pancakes, French toast, waffles, grits, eggs, bacon, sausage, ham, hash browns, toast and a choice of orange juice, coffee or water. But what stood out the most was the small, square, velvet box that sat directly in the center of the table amongst all of the food. McKinley couldn't believe her eyes. *I swear, if this is a joke I'ma kill'em,* she thought, picking up the box. Holding her breath, McKinley opened the box. Inside was a flawless, 5-carat, canary yellow, Harry Winston, square-cut diamond. The sight of the ring and the meaning behind it brought tears to her eyes.

"Baby," Jamil said from behind on one knee.

"Huh?" McKinley spun around swiftly.

"I know that we've had our ups and downs, but I love you and I don't wanna spend my life with anyone else, but you. Will you marry me?"

"Are you kidding me? Yes!" McKinley clasped her hands together and jumped up and down.

Jamil grinned. "Give me your hand."

McKinley extended her left hand and watched in awe as Jamil placed the ring on her finger.

"It's beautiful."

"You're beautiful." Jamil kissed the outside of her hand and stood up.

"I can't believe this is happening." McKinley wrapped her arms around Jamil's neck and squeezed him tight.

"I don't see why. You know that I love you."

"I know." She released her arms from around him and stepped back.

"It's just that—" She tried to speak, but couldn't because tears had started to rise in her throat.

"Stop." Jamil pulled her back into his embrace. "I know that things between us ain't always been good and that's mostly because of me. But on everything, I love you. I ain't on that shit no more. I'ma do right by you. Plus, I think it's time we start having some lil mini-mes runnin' around here." He picked her up in his arms and swung her around.

"You are crazy." McKinley giggled, feeling like she was about to burst from happiness.

Finally, everything she'd wished for was coming true. She'd prayed for years that this day would come. Jamil was the love of her life. Yes, he came with flaws, but who didn't? He loved her and she loved him. Anything her heart desired, he provided. Yes, because he was a drug dealer she often found herself at home alone, but to know that she would now have him to herself for the rest of her life was good enough for her.

"You love me?" Jamil placed her down and planted a deep kiss on her lips.

"Of course."

"Well, come show me how much then." He took her hand and led her back into the bedroom.

After spending the rest of the morning in bed, making love, McKinley fell asleep in Jamil's arms. Around one o'clock that afternoon McKinley opened her eyes once again to find herself in bed alone, except this time when she went searching the house for Jamil he was nowhere to be found. She did, however, find the living room filled with over five different bouquets of flowers.

"Awwwwwwwww." McKinley leaned over and inhaled the potent scent. "My day is just getting better and better." She gleamed with delight.

Seeing the sea of flowers warmed her heart. The gesture made her feel so special. She had to call Jamil to thank him. Using the cordless phone in the kitchen, she dialed his number. McKinley let the phone ring until his voicemail picked up.

"Hey, babe, thank you for the flowers. They're beautiful. I love them. I wish you would've told me you were leaving, but it's cool. I love you anyway. Just call me when you get this message."

XoXo

Distraught, McKinley paced back and forth across her living room floor in a purple maxi dress. Days had gone by and she hadn't heard from Jamil. She'd called him so much, the tips of her fingers were sore. Each time the phone would just ring and then go to voicemail. Sometimes her calls were forwarded to voicemail. She'd even tried texting him, but nothing worked. Jamil just wouldn't pick up the phone.

McKinley felt as if she'd been sucker-punched. It never failed, every time she got comfortable and made herself believe that things between them would be different, he always revealed his true self. She was so over the sleepless nights, broken promises, excuses and lame-ass apologies that came behind the wack-ass excuses. She desperately wanted to believe that the Jamil who looked her in the eyes and confessed his undying love, sang to her at night and even broke down in tears over her was the real him. But his actions kept showing her that he was an unreliable, selfish liar. He would continue to take her through unnecessary drama for the simple fact that he could. McKinley just prayed that he wasn't with another chick. She couldn't go through that kind of pain again.

"Has he ever done anything like this before?" Kristen asked, sitting on the couch Indian style.

"No." McKinley continued to pace the room. "The longest we've ever gone without speaking is maybe two days, but that's when we're mad at each other."

"Does he have a house phone at his apartment?"

"No, just his cell." McKinley massaged her forehead.

"You don't know any of his friends' numbers, so you can call and see if they've talked to him?" Kristen quizzed.

"No, and besides, Jamil would kill me if I called his friends lookin' for him," McKinley said, flushing in distress.

"Mmm." Kristen arched her eyebrow, shocked by her answer.

"Well, I don't know, friend." She picked up the bag of hot popcorn and resumed eating.

Not the one to give up, McKinley went to her contacts on her cell phone and pressed Jamil's name. After two rings she was forwarded to voicemail again.

"Oh, my God!" She mashed down the *End* button. "Like really? This nigga is straight up sending me to voicemail."

"Wow." Kristen shook her head.

"Like I swear to God I'ma fuck him up when I see him," McKinley fumed. "I mean like who proposes to someone then disappears for four days?"

"Jamil." Kristen couldn't help but laugh.

McKinley stopped mid-stride and glared at her.

"Word?" She shot Kristen a look that could kill.

"I'm sorry. You left yourself wide open for that one. Look," Kristen put down the bag of popcorn, "on the real, try callin' him one more time and if he doesn't answer then fuck it. Don't call his ass no more." She flicked her wrist.

"That's easier said then done," McKinley retorted indignantly. "This ain't just some nigga. This is the man I've been wit' for the last three years of my life. I can't just sit back not knowing whether he's dead or alive. What if something happened to him? Then what?" She threw her hands up in the air.

"You don't know his mama's number? I mean damn," Kristen responded, not knowing what else to do.

"No, they don't speak." McKinley ran her hands down her face.

"Then call him again, stalker." Kristen rolled her eyes and took a sip of her soda.

McKinley eagerly dialed Jamil's number, praying this time he would answer.

"Hello?" A little boy answered the phone.

"Uhhhhhhhhhhhhhhhhhh." McKinley took the phone away from her ear to make sure she'd dialed the right number. "Is Jamil there?"

"This is me," the little boy replied, cheerfully.

"No, sweetie, I'm looking for Jamil," McKinley repeated, but in a louder tone as if the boy was deaf.

"This is me, silly lady." The boy chuckled.

"Ummm," McKinley looked at Kristen confused, "is your daddy there?" she probed.

"Are you serious?" Kristen mouthed.

"Yeah. You wanna talk to him? 'Cause he makin' me a peanut butter and jelly sandwich right now," the boy said.

"Yes. Can you put him on the phone?" McKinley asked, feeling faint.

"Okay." The boy put down the phone. "Daddy. Telephone."

"What?" McKinley swore she heard Jamil say in the background.

The next thing she knew the phone went dead and she was left with silence. Shocked by what just took place, she stood paralyzed in the center of the floor.

"What happened?" Kristen asked, genuinely concerned.

Anxiety was written all over McKinley's face.

"Some lil boy answered the phone," McKinley responded in a daze, "and he said that his name was Jamil. I asked him to put his daddy on the phone and the boy said okay. Then the boy called out for his daddy, and I swear, Kristen, I heard Jamil say 'what' in the background." Her eyes bucked.

"Hell naw," Kristen said, dumbfounded. "So you really think it was Jamil?"

"Who else could it have been?" McKinley checked the number she'd dialed to confirm it. "The proof is right here." She showed Kristen her phone. "I dialed the right number, so it had to have been him."

"How old did the lil boy sound?"

"At least about five." McKinley shrugged her shoulders dismissively.

"Girl, this is too much for me. This is the type of shit you read about in one of them Keisha Ervin novels." Kristen waved her hand and got up. "I need a drink. You mind if I open up a bottle of wine?"

"No." McKinley walked over to the couch and sat down in a haze.

Seconds later, Kristen came back with a bottle of wine and two glasses.

"Here." Kristen handed McKinley a glass of Pinot. "This will make you feel better."

McKinley took a long sip then looked at Kristen, and said, "What if this nigga got a baby?"

"Don't even claim that. It could've been his nephew, cousin, anybody," Kristen reasoned, praying to God she was right.

McKinley sat with the glass of wine in her hand, gazing blankly at the floor. It was time for her to leave Jamil alone. Holding onto him wasn't healthy. Child or no child, he'd told one too many lies and let her down too many times for her to continue to give him chance after chance. It was time for her to accept that this was who he was. She just couldn't figure out what the tears and long heartfelt conversations that lasted until the wee hours of the morning were for. None of it made sense.

Why did he profusely profess his love for her only to break her heart over and over again? Was it all a game that she didn't know she was participating in? The only thing she knew for sure was that she was tired of playing the guessing game. It was time for McKinley to put an end to the madness, even if it meant her heart breaking in the process. After finishing a whole bottle of Pinot, and hours of discussing the situation with Kristen, both women became tired.

Kristen yawned. "I am exhausted."

McKinley exhaled. "Me, too."

Even after all of the talking they'd done, her stomach was still in knots.

"You want me to spend the night?" Kristen asked, stretching.

"Nah, I'll be okay." McKinley fiddled with her fingers.

"You sure? 'Cause I will stay if you want me to."

"I'm good." McKinley stood up and stretched her legs. "Go to your apartment and get some rest. I've taken up enough of your time as it is." She forced herself to smile.

"Girl, please, I ain't have shit else to do. Besides, you're my girl and you would've done the same thing for me. Hell, you *have* done the same thing for me." Kristen laughed.

"You silly." McKinley laughed, too.

"Well, look, call me if you need me." Kristen gave McKinley a warm hug.

"I will, and thanks again." McKinley hugged her back, then opened the door.

"No problem. Now go to sleep. Don't call him no more. You're only going to make yourself feel worse."

"I won't." McKinley assured, closing and locking the door behind her.

Alone, she placed her back against the door and took in the silence. The sound was excruciating. McKinley hated that she was going through this shit. It wasn't fair. She'd loved Jamil with every fiber of her being. She'd given him her all. She'd stood by his side through the good and the bad. When he fucked up, she was the one to pick up the pieces.

When he was afraid, she calmed his fears, but when she needed him, he was always unavailable. The whole situation was fucked up. Every time she thought they were making progress he always took ten steps backward, crushing her heart in two. It fucked her up that he wasn't emotionally responsible with her heart.

Time and time again Jamil would fill her heart with words of hope that he'd change and be a better man, and each time his actions proved differently. McKinley didn't know whether to believe his intentions or the outcome of his actions. It was all mind-numbing—loving someone who held her heart on a string like a Marionette.

McKinley needed answers and fast. She needed to know what was going on with him and why he was being so insensitive of her feelings. It was obvious he was alive and well because she hadn't heard differently. Jamil was simply ignoring her, and the sad part was he didn't even have a reason to.

He was just selfish and until he decided to give up an explanation that was just how it was. Tired of debating with herself, McKinley wearily walked over to the stairs. She didn't know if she'd be able to sleep or not, but she had to lie down. McKinley didn't even make it up the steps before she heard the distinct sound of the front door opening.

Quickly, she spun around. Her heart was beating out of her chest in anticipation of seeing his face. Then he walked through the door. She could smell the enthralling scent of his Dolce & Gabbana cologne all the way from across the room. He looked better than he had the last time she saw him, crushing her spirit even more.

Jamil looked absolutely divine in a yellow BLVCK SCVLE T-shirt, Altamont fitted jeans and a brand new pair of $700 Dior Homme sneakers. McKinley was relieved to see that he was well, but confirmation of that signified her worst fear that he'd been dodging her on purpose.

She stormed down the steps. "Where in the hell have you been?"

"Calm down."

She pointed her index finger like a gun at his forehead. "Fuck that! Ain't no calming down!"

"Why the fuck haven't you been answering your phone? I've been callin' you for days. I thought you were dead. But no, you're alive and well. So you've been sending me to voicemail all this time like I ain't shit?" She got up in his face.

"Like I'm not yo' fiancée or should I give the ring back?" McKinley pulled off her ring and threw at him. "'Cause apparently the ring don't mean a damn thing."

"Will you let me explain?" Jamil tried reaching out for her, but McKinley snatched her hand away and shot him a look that could kill.

"Don't touch me. Touch whoever you don' been wit' the last couple of days. Wit' yo' lousy ass! And who the fuck is Jamil?"

"What?" Jamil eyed her, confused.

"Nigga, don't act stupid. I called your phone and some boy named Jamil picked up the phone." McKinley rolled her neck. "Don't lie to me. Tell the truth. You gotta a kid?"

"Man, I ain't come over here to talk about no kid." Jamil shook his head, never once giving her eye contact.

"What you mean you don't wanna talk about no kid? I dialed the right number, Jamil, and I swear I heard you talkin' in the background." McKinley's voice cracked.
"You know what? I don't even know why the fuck I bother." Jamil's nostrils flared. "This why I can't never talk to you 'cause you always on some other shit. You always assuming the worst. I know, I'm wrong. I don't ever do shit right. What's new? Shit, fuck this, I'm up." He turned to leave.

McKinley knew she should've called his bluff and let him walk out the door, but the part of her heart that needed him more than she needed air to breathe wouldn't allow it.

"Jamil, wait." She jumped in front of him and blocked his path.

"Nah." He shook his head. "I'm tired of this shit. I came over here to talk to you. Not be accused of a bunch of foul shit."

McKinley gazed into his eyes. A world of pain hid behind his irises. She wondered how long it had been lying there. She'd never seen Jamil look so sad before. She felt like shit. Maybe she had overreacted? Maybe the boy who answered his phone had been his cousin?

"Will you calm down? I just don't understand what's going on."

"Okay, but instead of jumpin' to conclusions, how about you listen to me sometimes."

"I'm sorry." McKinley shrugged her shoulders and shook her head.

"I'm for real, McKinley. Don't come to me on no shit like this again. You gotta learn how to trust me. I got enough on my plate as it is." Jamil turned his face and looked away, mad.

McKinley stuck her face in front of his. "I understand. I was just worried about you."

"I don't even wanna talk about that no more. Just come lay down wit' me. I'm tired and I wanna lie down," he said, going up the stairs.

McKinley followed Jamil to her bedroom. Once there, she climbed into bed while he took off his sneakers. Once his shoes were off, Jamil got into bed and lay behind her. His strong arms enveloped her waist. Jamil placed a soft kiss on the nape of her neck.

"I love you," he whispered.

"I love you, too," McKinley said reluctantly.

Sure, this was the side of Jamil she loved; it was just sad he couldn't be this way all the time. McKinley just couldn't allow herself to fall back into the same routine just 'cause the touch of his hand on her skin made her feel alive. This shit had to stop. She was tired of feeling like she was the only one dying. No way could he disappear for four days and this be it.

"Uh ah." She shot up.

There was no way she could just lay down and pretend that the last four days hadn't happened.

"I can't do this."
"Do what?" Jamil mumbled.

"I can't do *this* anymore." McKinley stressed the word this.

"What's wrong wit' you now, McKinley?" Jamil huffed, opening his eyes.

"I'll tell you exactly what's wrong with me. I'm tired of you doing whatever the fuck you wanna do, then when I step to you about it you flip out on me and make it seem like *I'm* crazy. I know what happened. It's not okay that you do this kind of stuff and I just sit here and fuckin' take it."

"C'mon, babe. I'm tired, just lay down. We'll talk about this in the morning." Jamil tried to get her to lie back down.

"No, I don't wanna lay down, and we gon' talk about this right now," she hissed, pushing him away.

"I want you to explain to me how you can propose to me and disappear on me all in the same damn day. What kind of shit is that and who does shit like that? You claim to love me so much, but every chance you get you're hurtin' me. And I don't understand why you do me like this." McKinley began to cry. "Oh, I know why. You do it 'cause you can."

"Stop." Jamil sat up and tried to hold her, but McKinley wasn't willing to let her defenses down.

"No! If we're gonna get married I need for you to change. I'm tired of yo' mouth making promises, but your actions showing me something different. I'm tired of one minute we're good and then within a blink of an eye it's some bullshit all over again. This shit is driving me insane."
"I told you I was gonna change. But change takes time, McKinley. You gotta give me a chance to do it," Jamil reasoned.

"I've given you three years to change. If it ain't happened by now then it ain't gon' happen," McKinley shrieked.

"So what you sayin'?"

McKinley sat quietly and collected herself.

"I think we need to take a break," she finally said.

"A break?" Jamil looked at her sideways. "What the fuck you mean, 'a break'? We ain't takin' no fuckin' break? If we ain't gon' be together, we ain't gon' be together. Ain't no in-between."

"Then I guess we ain't gon' be together then," McKinley replied calmly.

"Word? So that's it?" Jamil stared at her surprised.

"Yeah."

"A'ight." Jamil got out of the bed and put on his shoes.

McKinley willed herself to breathe. With each second that passed, it seemed like she was going to faint. Her stomach was in knots as she watched Jamil grab his keys. If she wanted him now was the time to stop him, but the further he got down the hall the firmer she stood on her decision. This would be good for the both of them. McKinley just prayed that her walking away wouldn't be the biggest mistake of her life.

"The problem is that you know where my heart stands. You use it against me."

Dawn Richards
"Broken Record"

When she'd made it up in her mind that leaving Jamil alone was the right move to make, McKinley never considered the fact that being without him would cause more than a broken heart. Being without Jamil made her feel like she'd died one hundred times. Everyday was like Groundhog's Day. Every morning she relived the fact that he was gone and never coming back. She would never hear the sound of his footsteps coming up the steps.

She wouldn't feel him lying next to her in the middle of the night. She wouldn't get to smell the sweet scent of his skin. The sound of his laughter wouldn't fill the house up anymore. Every moment of the day she spent alone. When the phone rang everything in her hoped that it would be him on the other end, begging for her forgiveness. She'd called him and left him messages, begging him to call her, but Jamil hadn't called once.

It had been two weeks since she heard his voice or saw his face. It was like he'd fallen off the face of the earth. Curled up in bed, McKinley gazed at the wall. Tears slid out of the corners of her eyes at a rapid speed. She'd hardly eaten in days. When she closed her eyes at night the only thing she dreamed of was him. No matter what she did, thoughts of Jamil haunted her brain.

Her friends said that in time the pain would get better, but McKinley didn't believe it. To be without Jamil was worse than being with him. The inconsistencies of their relationship she could handle, but the constant pang in her heart was torture. She wanted her baby back. Everyone around her would call her dumb, but she didn't care. They weren't the ones suffering.

McKinley didn't know what to do. Begging him to take her back made her feel like a complete and utter fool, but every second she breathed air knowing he wasn't hers anymore killed her. Fuck pride, McKinley had to get her man back. Using her cell phone, she called him. Each ring felt like death. It hurt her even more when he didn't pick up.

McKinley hung up the phone and burst into tears. *How can he just ignore me like this,* she wondered when her phone rang. McKinley looked at the screen. It was Jamil. A sense of relief flooded over her body.

"Hello?" Her voice quivered.

"What's up? You called?" he asked nonchalantly.

McKinley could hear music and people talking in the background. It sounded as if he was at club or a bar.

"Yeah, you know I did," she answered with a slight attitude.

"Look, I ain't call you to argue."

"I didn't call you to argue either," McKinley explained.

"Well, what's up then?" Jamil asked dryly.

"Will you please come home? I'm sorry. I made a mistake. I thought that breaking up wit' you was the best thing to do, but it was not. I miss you," she cried. "And I just want you to come home."

"I don't know if I can do that," Jamil said regrettably.

"Why?" McKinley said taken aback by his answer. "'Cause, man. You were right. We needed to fall back from each other. And I mean, I miss you and everything, but I don't think we ready to just jump back into being wit' each other."

"That's a bunch of bullshit and you know it," McKinley cried out. "I love you and you love me."

"I never said that I didn't love you. Love just don't go away overnight," Jamil confessed.

"So that's it? You just don't wanna be wit' me no more." McKinley stopped crying.

"I ain't tryin' to be rude or nothin', but can I call you back?"

McKinley held the phone stunned.

"Hello?" Jamil said.

"Yeah," she replied, feeling like if she let him get off the phone she'd never hear from him again.

"Can I call you right back?"

"Whatever, Jamil." McKinley rolled her eyes and hung up the phone.

"What the hell am I sittin' up here cryin' over this nigga for?" McKinley said out loud to herself, pissed off.

Fed up, she got out of the bed and turned on the light.

"The hell with this shit," she spat. "I'm sittin' over her feeling like I'm dying and this nigga could care less, he out partying. Fuck this."

McKinley went into the master bathroom and looked at herself in the mirror. She looked a mess. She hadn't combed her hair in days. Her face looked pale and dry. Dried-up tear stains scarred her cheeks. Tired of looking and feeling disgusted, she turned on the shower and got in. The hot water running over her body made her feel as if she was being hugged.

Once her body was clean and fresh she turned off the water and got out. After drying off, McKinley brushed her teeth and washed her face, then grabbed her Wild Cherry Blossom lotion and walked back into her room. Annoyed with the silence that enveloped her, she popped a mix CD into her Blu Ray player. The first song that began to play was Jazmine Sullivan's fuck-him-girl anthem "Holding You Down." McKinley sat on the edge of her bed and began lathering on lotion while singing along.

It's a shame that you don't care enough,

To even give me half the love,

I give to you,

I live for you baby,

I'm ashamed to say that I'm to blame for how you act,

'Cause I keep comin' back.

McKinley couldn't sing a lick, but every lyric from the song resonated deep within her soul. After every inch of her skin was covered with lotion, McKinley went over to her walk-in closet and pulled out the most uncomplicated outfit she could find. Then Barbra Streisand's "Don't Rain on My Parade," from the iconic movie, *Funny Girl,* came on.

Don't tell me not to live,

Just sit and putter,

Life's candy and the suns a ball of butter.

She stood up and danced like a Broadway dancer.

Fuck staying in the house sulking. It was time for her to live. She wasn't going to let Jamil rain on her parade. He was living and going on with his life, so why shouldn't she make the same moves? Dressed in a Camilla and Marc, print Georgette dress with a scoop neck, cutout shoulders and short flutter sleeves, McKinley placed on a cute pair of gold sandals.

Standing in front of the mirror, she pulled her hair up into a sleek ponytail, dabbed on a little pink lip gloss, grabbed her house keys and headed out the door. But to McKinley's surprise as soon as she stepped out of the door, Jamil got off the elevator. McKinley stood frozen, wondering could he hear the loud thumping in her chest that sounded like a drum beat.

"Where you going?" he asked, eying her up and down.

"Why?" McKinley replied.

She didn't want to tell him the truth, which was she had no idea where she was going.

"'Cause I want you to take a walk with me," Jamil said.

McKinley looked away; hating that Jamil's presence had such an impact on her. Every time she came near him her entire being was reduced to a mere puddle. Her mouth begged her to tell him to kick rocks, but the pull he had on her heartstrings triumphed and she found herself saying, "Okay."

In a daze, McKinley boarded the elevator with Jamil in silence. She was all prepared to say fuck him and to start moving on with her life. But just like every other time she was ready to take that step into the unknown, Jamil appeared, causing her to steer off course. Outside the cool night air kissed their skin as they walked side by side down the street.

"So what do you wanna talk to me about?" McKinley said at once.

"I wanted to tell you that I'm sorry. I know that I haven't treated you right, but I'm tryin', McKinley. I love you and I don't wanna lose you."

"I can't tell. I haven't heard from you in two weeks," McKinley said simply.

"And by no means necessary do I want you to think that was easy for me. I'm fucked up by this, too. I haven't been able to sleep at night," he confessed.

"Well, how come when I called you, you didn't answer the phone?" she countered.

"I mean, what was I gon' say? What I did was fucked up and nothin' I said was gon' make you feel any better, so I just decided to fall back for a minute."

McKinley took in his words and let them digest in her brain. She desperately wanted to believe what he was telling her, but she'd heard this same speech one too many times before to trust in his word.

"So what now?" she asked, walking at a slow pace.

"If you allow me the chance, I wanna show you that I can be everything you need me to be and more," Jamil said after a pause.

McKinley closed her eyes and inhaled deeply. She'd prayed to God repeatedly to stop the nagging pain that lay in the center of her chest. Now was her chance to end it. This was it, after this, Jamil would get no more chances. If he didn't get it right this time then she was done for good.

"I'll give you another chance, but if you don't do right by me this time, I'm done," she said with a sudden fierceness.

"I swear to *God*, this time it's gon' be different," Jamil assured, smoothing back her hair.

McKinley relished his touch and said a silent prayer to God that this time the desires of her heart would come to fruition.

XoXo

It was the middle of summer and McKinley was on cloud nine. She and Jamil had been getting along tremendously. They hadn't fought one time. Jamil had been on his best behavior.

He'd become more attentive. He catered to her every whim. Whatever free time he had to spare when he wasn't working was spent with her. He'd even been assisting with the wedding plans.

Two hundred and fifty of their closest family and friends would attend their nuptials. Their wedding date had been set for September 8. McKinley couldn't wait to become Mrs. Jamil Thompson. Her first duty as his wife would be to give him the son that he'd always wanted. That day after meeting with their wedding planner and going over table settings and centerpieces, McKinley hopped into her Mercedes G Wagon and headed back home to meet up with Jamil.

They were going to go over the seating chart. It had been hell trying to figure out where to seat everyone. As McKinley pulled up to her building, her cell phone began to ring. It was Jamil. A huge smile spread across her face.

"Hey, baby," she said, parking her car.

"Where you at?" he asked.

"Just pulling up to the house, why? Where are you?" she asked, turning off the ignition.

"Please don't be mad, but I'm runnin' a lil bit behind."

"How behind, Jamil?" McKinley groaned.

"Like an hour."

"Are you kidding me? I just rushed home, thinkin' I was gon' meet you here."

"My bad. I'ma be there as soon as I can," he promised.

"Okay, Jamil, hurry up," McKinley insisted.

"I am."

"All right, love you," she uttered.

"Love you, too."

Since Jamil would be arriving late, McKinley decided to take matters into her own hands and start doing the seating charts on her own. She had no time to waste. Every second of the day counted. Plus, she had a million other things that needed to be completed as well. She couldn't put the seating charts off another day.

Once the elevator doors opened, McKinley stormed into her apartment on a mission. Dropping her bags at the door, she quickly began creating the perfect seating chart. Almost two hours later she'd only gotten two of the tables done and was past frustrated. Annoyed that Jamil hadn't showed up yet, she texted him.

To: Jamil
Where are you?
Sent:
Fri, Aug 12, 4:50 pm

To: McKinley
I'ma b there in a min.

Received:
Mon, Aug 12, 4:52 pm

To: Jamil
What's a min, Jamil?
Sent:
Mon, Aug 12, 4:54 pm

To: McKinley
Half an hour
Received:
Mon, Aug 12, 5:01 pm

Overwhelmed, McKinley threw down her phone and went over to the refrigerator. Her stomach was growling so loud it sounded like she'd passed gas. Needing something quick and fresh to eat, she fixed herself a ham sandwich with celery sticks and peanut butter on the side. Trying her best not to focus on the time, McKinley sat at the dining room table and ate her food while watching *Dancing with the Stars*. Before she knew it, she'd finished eating, the program had gone off and Jamil still hadn't shown up. Fed up, she dialed his number.

"What's up?" Jamil said in a low tone.

"I cannot believe you starting this shit again. I've been sittin' here, waitin' on you all afternoon. Where the fuck are you?" McKinley yelled.

"Yo, I can't be talkin' to you right now."

"What you say?" McKinley replied, taken aback.

"Let me call you back. I'm in the middle of something."

"Jamil, I swear to God if you hang up this phone I'm officially done fuckin' wit' you," McKinley warned.

"Babe, just give me a minute," he pleaded.

But before McKinley could reply the sound of gun fire caused her heart to leap out of her chest and fall flat onto the floor.

"Jamil." She called out for him but got no reply.

"Jamil," she screamed, praying to God he'd answer.

"Jamil!"

Part Two

"And the anger and the sorrow mixed up leaves the mistrust. Now it gets tough to ever love again."

Jay Z
"Allure"

McKinley had worn the same clothes for two days. She sat Indian style, in the center of her king-sized bed, clutching Jamil's pillow, wishing that he was there. It was the middle of the night, but so what? Sleep had become an insufferable pastime she could do without. A pain so strong resonated from her ribs and through her eyes, causing an abundance of tears to stream down her face. He was gone and with each second that passed by that conclusion became clearer. She wished this time was like the other times they'd fought and he'd left.

She'd cry until her throat was sore, he'd come back, rock her pussy to sleep, then promise that everything would be okay. But two days ago, everything changed. He was brutally gunned down outside of his apartment and she was forced to deal with the fact that this time he was gone for good. She would never feel his lips on hers or have the pleasure of being wrapped in his warm embrace. All of her days from now on would be long, drawn out and insignificant. She'd forever be chasing pavements, instead of obsessing over him.

"It's not fair," she sobbed, hitting his pillow with her fist.

It wasn't fair that they never got to say good-bye with words. It wasn't fair that he was killed for reasons unknown. And it most certainly wasn't fair that she sat alone, gazing at a picture of him, wondering why he couldn't be a part of her future. Doubled over in pain, McKinley cried tears of sorrow and loneliness. The 5-carat canary-yellow diamond ring, closet full of designer shoes and dresses and Hermes Birkin bags wouldn't comfort her in her time of need.

McKinley would give it all, her heart, her home, her clothes, anything she owned just to have him back. Reluctantly, she let go of the pillow and placed her face into her hands. An eerie quietness surrounded her. Just as she was about to release a blood-curdling scream to the heavens up above, a thunderous bang came crashing through her front door. Scared out of her mind, she sat frozen stiff. From her bedroom she could hear the sound of heavy footsteps run rampant throughout her apartment.

Suddenly, the door to her bedroom swung open. Five men dressed in black charged inside with flashlights pointing her way. McKinley turned her face and lifted her arm to shield her eyes from the blaring lights.

"Freeze! Put your hands behind your head and stand against the wall," the federal agent ordered.

"What the hell are you all doing in my house?" McKinley demanded to know, ignoring their orders.

"Ma'am, I'm only going to ask you one more time. Please get off of the bed."

"Not until you tell me what the fuck—"

Before McKinley knew it, her bedroom light was on and her petite body was being dragged from the bed and placed up against the wall. McKinley let out a scream for help so loud she swore her neighbors would hear.

"Shut up!" the man ordered.

"What the hell is going on?" she demanded to know.

"We have a warrant to search your place—"

"Sir, we found a safe," one of the agents said, pulling a silver safe from out of the floor.

"And we're bringing you in for questioning," the federal agent explained.

"But I didn't do anything. What is going on?" she wailed.

McKinley was so incoherent that she didn't even realize she'd been spun around. Everything was moving so fast she felt high. The federal agents walked past her in slow motion as if she wasn't even there. McKinley stood back and watched helplessly with tears in her eyes as they ransacked her place. The Matteograssi bed that she and Jamil slept in, made love in, shared dreams in was broken down.

The Ligne Roset side table he used to place his cell phone on at night was turned over as if it wasn't worth anything. The federal agents searched relentlessly for some kind of evidence she didn't know existed. The very pillow she held close to her heart a second ago was ripped down the middle, exposing a wealth of white feathers. Some of Jamil's jewelry and clothes that he kept there were thrown on the floor.

"The safe is filled with money," one of the agents informed his captain.

"What is going on? What are you looking for?"

"Okay, men, we've found what we need. Let's wrap this up. Agent Franklin, take this young lady down to the car. She's coming with us."

XoXo

"Thanks for coming to get me." McKinley massaged her wrists, coming out of the federal building.

Kristen wrapped her arm around McKinley's shoulder. "Are you okay?"

McKinley threw up her arms. "No, look at me."

Kristen hated to admit it, but McKinley looked horrible. Dried tears stained her caramel face. Her hair was all over her head. The

Jill Stuart silk chiffon print maxi dress with a ruffle overlay at the bodice and cascading ruffles at the skirt that she'd worn two days before was a worn and tattered mess. Kristen could even smell a foul stench come from her body.

"Kristen, I don't know what I'm going to do," McKinley explained, getting into the car.

"I ain't tryin' to be funny, but do you mind if we let the window down?" Kristen held her nose.

"Fuck you, bitch. I know I stink."

"Hey, I'm just sayin'. I need to have a clear mind while I drive." Kristen laughed.

"All jokes aside," McKinley said seriously. "Shit is fucked up. They've seized all of our accounts. I don't have a dime to my name."

"For real?"

"You think I'm playin'?"

"Damn," Kristen said as she drove back to their apartment.

"I can't believe this shit is happening to me." McKinley stared out the window wearily.

"Everything's gonna be all right, McKinley. I got a little stash of money put up. It's not much, but I'll help you the best that I can." Kristen pulled into her personal parking space.

"No, Kristen. I can't take money from you."

"Girl, please. You're my best friend. I ain't gon' let you go without."

"Thank you." McKinley gave her a slight smile.

After saying hello to the doorman, McKinley and Kristen boarded the elevator in silence. Once at her door, McKinley inhaled deeply and prepared herself for the worst. Gradually, she pushed open the door. Her living room was a wreck. The curtains were pulled. Mirrors were broken. Cushions from the couch were slit open and thrown about. The coffee table was turned over. Papers were sprawled all over the floor. McKinley could only imagine what the rest of the place looked like.

"Muthafuckin' cocksuckers," she yelled, pissed.

"I can't believe they did this." Kristen gazed around, amazed by the carnage.

"This is some bullshit," McKinley exclaimed, running from room to room.

Carefully, Kristen picked up a black-and-white photo of McKinley that was on the floor. Jamil had taken it while they were on vacation in St. Bart's two summers ago. In the photo McKinley smiled gleefully. Rays from the sun shined down onto her honey-colored skin. McKinley looked strikingly beautiful in the picture.

"They straight fucked up all of my shit. What the fuck am I going to do?" McKinley reentered the living area.

"Okay, I know it's a lot, but just calm down." Kristen placed the picture on top of the mantle. "So what now?" Kristen asked.

"Shit, I don't know. You tell me. I'm a broke, twenty-five-year-old woman with hardly any work experience and not a pot to piss in. My fiancé is dead. I mean, how could my life get any worse?"

The words hadn't even settled into the atmosphere before there was a loud knock on McKinley's door.

"You expecting company?" Kristen turned and looked at her.

"No. It's probably one of the neighbors. They've been bringing food and flowers all week," McKinley said, slowly easing up from the floor. "Who is it?"

"Leah."

McKinley gazed over her shoulder at Kristen with a perplexed expression on her face. She didn't know anyone named Leah. Slowly, she unlocked the door and found a well-dressed woman who looked to be in her mid-thirties, standing there.

"May I help you?" McKinley asked politely with her hand on the knob.

"McKinley, right?" Leah asked, clutching her Carlos Falchi clutch purse.

"And you are?" McKinley ignored her question, afraid she might be a detective.

"Leah Thompson…Jamil's wife."

The only thing McKinley could do was chuckle. *This chick is clearly delusional,* she thought. *There is no way on God's green earth that my Jamil was married, especially not to this chick. Hell, I have been with him for three years, so where in the hell has this chick been the whole time? 'Cause he was here with me at least four to five days out of the week. Yeah, this bitch is crazy, so let me shut this chick down like a bad Ferris wheel, so I can get back to being depressed.*

"Look, lady, I don't know who you are, but——"

"As I stated before, I'm his wife," Leah said with an even tone. "So to make this as simple as possible, let me get you up to speed.

Jamil and I have been married for nine years and we have two lovely children, Brianna and Jamil Jr."

McKinley immediately remembered the phone call where the lil boy answered the phone. *So that was his son,* she thought.

"We have a home, or shall I say, a mansion on Star Island, and an apartment in Tribeca, New York, and a beach house in Malibu. I've known about you for about two years now."

"So why are you just sayin' something now?" McKinley snapped.

"'Cause you weren't the first woman he stepped out on me with and you for damn sure weren't the last. To be exact, it's me, then his other girlfriend slash baby mama Tanay, then you. And yes, to be clear, he was seeing all three of us at the same time. Did it hurt in the beginning, yes? Do I care now, no? 'Cause I knew this day would come where I would get everything."

McKinley stood speechless. She hadn't even blinked she was so stunned.

"Yeah, I know it's a shock. It was also a shock to me when I found out that he'd proposed to you with a five-carat diamond ring a couple of months ago and you tearfully said yes," Leah said mockingly.

"Oh, but wait, there's more. Because of my husband's untimely passing, I now have to tie up all of his loose ends. See, this fairly modest apartment that you've been living in is under Jamil's name and since I'm his beneficiary I now have control of it. So I've decided to sell this apartment immediately, which gives you thirty days to vacate the premises."

"What? You've got to be kidding, right?" McKinley said in disbelief.

"No, honey, sorry, I'm not. Well, look, now that we've gotten a chance to chat I have to be off. I do have a funeral to plan." Leah secured her purse underneath her arm. "It was nice meeting you, McKinley. I wish you the best of luck. Smooches." Leah blew McKinley a kiss then sashayed off down the hallway.

"What was that all about?" Kristen asked standing up.

"Oh, just the usual, you know," McKinley scoffed. "That was Jamil's wife. She came by to tell me that I have thirty days to vacate the premises. So I guess I was wrong. My life *can* get worse."

"O...M...G, really?" Kristen said, aghast.

"Yes. This whole time that muthafucka was living a double life. Here I am thinking I'm the only one and he got a whole wife, two kids *and* a baby mama. I was with him for three years and all I have to show for it is a bunch of clothes and a wack-ass engagement ring. This bitch gets everything and I'm left with nothing. I gave up my family and my friends for him. He had me thinkin' we were gon' be together forever." McKinley cried hysterically.

"So what are you going to do?"

McKinley stood, trembling with fear. There was only one way out of her predicament. The one thing she'd been dreading the most. The word alone made her cringe and brought on bouts of anxiety.

"I guess I'll have to," she swallowed hard, "go home."

"I guess I met you for a reason. Only time can tell."

J Cole feat Drake
"In The Morning"

After two weeks of packing up her things and having them shipped to St. Louis, courtesy of her mother, it was time for McKinley to bid farewell. It was her last day in Miami before flying home to St. Louis. She'd truly miss Miami. She didn't know how she'd live without the smell of sea salt or seeing the leaves from the palm trees sway in the wind. She'd yearn for the scrumptious food, colorful printed clothes, all-night club scene and great weather. More then anything she'd miss all of the time she and Jamil spent there.

When they'd met three years prior, while she was on vacation, he'd swept her off her feet and she'd never left. Now she was being forced to leave. Parts of her hated him for the lies he'd told and for making her feel like she was the only one. But for the last three years of her life all she'd known was the love he'd shown her.

After strolling the beach one last time, McKinley placed her orange, suede, peep- toe heels back on and headed to Hotel Victor for an early dinner. As she walked the sun was just starting to set when suddenly she spotted him. There he was, sitting on the edge of his silver, SL 65 AMG, with his left hand in his pocket, surrounded by his homeboys. Everything about him screamed heartbreaker and to keep it moving, but McKinley couldn't take her eyes off of him.

He was six feet, 190 pounds with skin the color of peanut butter. A blue Yankee's cap cocked to the left covered his low cut, but enhanced his Asian-inspired eyes, chiseled cheekbones and soft kissable lips. She didn't know if he had a girl, but visions of what they could be filled her mind. He was the type of nigga she wanted to wake up in the morning and cook breakfast for, forget her past for, shed tears for; but McKinley had bigger fish to fry. Like figuring out where she'd get her next buck from. Using the common sense God gave her, she made her way into the hotel's lobby instead of giving into temptation.

Hotel Victor was one of South Beach's premier hotels. Their luxury suites, breathtaking views and spa treatments were one of a kind. McKinley especially loved their use of vibrant colors and modern furniture. Vix wasn't just another South Beach restaurant, it was an experience. It provided artistry in every aspect of the restaurant, from the cuisine to their elegant paintings. The tables were made of beautiful marble slabs. Each one was stylishly decorated with vanilla tea candles and twenty-four karat flatware. There were a mixture of crème and mustard colored chairs, trimmed in brown. McKinley was seated at a table for two by the window, which was opened.

A soothing breeze kissed her skin as she skimmed through the menu. Once her order was placed McKinley pulled out her cell to call her mother, but the sight of Jamil's face on her screen brought her to tears. Overthrown with emotions, she threw the phone back inside her purse as well as her ring. She couldn't imagine what her life would be like now that Jamil was dead.

Not only was he her boyfriend, but her mentor and friend; so when the proposal of marriage came up, there was no way she could say no. But now, McKinley was on her own and with little to no money and forced to move back in with her mother. Unknowingly a tear slipped from her eye and she began to cry. Choking back the tears that filled her throat, McKinley got up and walked quickly to the restroom to gather her emotions.

Once her emotions were in check she placed on a new coat of Chanel lip gloss and exited the restroom. On her way back to her table she locked eyes with the caramel thug from outside. Pleased to see her again, he strolled toward her with a smile. McKinley hoped and prayed that he couldn't tell she'd been crying as he approached.

"How you doing?" He gently took her hand, fascinated by her facial features.

"Fine and you?" McKinley smiled.

"Better now."

"Really?" She laughed.

"Yeah. So what's your name?"

"McKinley."

"Nice to meet you McKinley." He looked at her in awe.

"Nice to meet you, too. . ."

"Koran." He shook his head.

"My bad. It's just that you look like someone I used to know." Koran referred to his late wife, Whitney, who had lost her battle with cancer three years before.

If it wasn't for the height and weight difference, McKinley would've been a dead ringer for Whitney.

"I get that a lot." McKinley chuckled.

"So umm. . .are you here with somebody?" Koran looked around. "I don't wanna get you in trouble or nothin'," he joked.

"You good, no actually, I'm here by myself." McKinley stared him directly in the eye while still holding onto his hand.

"That's what's up." Koran nodded. "So uh . . .you gon' let my hand go or what?"

"Oh, I'm sorry." McKinley drew her hand back and blushed.

"It's all good. I was just fuckin' wit' you. Were you on your way out or have you already been seated?"

"I've already been seated. I was just on my way back to my table."

"You need someone to go wit' you," Koran flirted.
"If you want to."

"So, McKinley, what's a pretty girl like you doing walkin' down the streets of Miami by yourself this time of the day? It's a lot of bad guys out here. You gotta be safe."

"Are you one of the bad guys or are you a bad guy tryin' to be good?"

"I guess you could say I'm a little bit of both. Hopefully you'll stick around long enough to find out."

"Maybe I will."

Koran normally wasn't the type of dude to go after a female so hard, but he had to get to know the woman who resembled his late wife. Besides that, there was something about McKinley that told him she needed a real man in her life. She'd caught his attention as soon as she turned the corner. At that moment he knew he had to holla at her. She was stunningly beautiful, but in her own unique way. Due to the warm Miami heat, she wore a ribbed cashmere polo shirt and a pair of silk twill Louis Vuitton shorts. A topaz and gold braid necklace with black diamonds designed by Janis Savitt completed her look. Girlfriend was fly and from the way she talked, it seemed like she had her mind right.

"So, Koran, do you live here?" McKinley quizzed.

"Nah, I just came here for a wedding."

"Excuse me, sir, would you like something to drink?" a server asked.

"Yeah, I'll have whatever she's having," Koran replied.

"You might not want to do that." McKinley snickered.

"Why not?" Koran eyed her perplexed.

"I'm having a shot of Patron."

"Man, please, you made it seem like you was talkin' about something." He waved her off. "I'll have two shots of Patron," he said to the waiter.

"Bring me out another as well," McKinley said to the server, too.

"So this how we doing it?" Koran grinned.

"Might as well," McKinley shrugged her shoulders.

Seconds later their waiter returned with their drinks and placed them on the table before them.

"Okay, here we go." McKinley held up her shot glass.

"Cheers!" Koran tapped his glass against hers then quickly guzzled it down.

McKinley did the same.

"Whew," she grimaced, shaking her head.

"You think you can handle another?" Koran smiled mischievously.

"I can handle anything you can dish out."

XoXo

The following morning McKinley awoke in a drunken haze. Lying on her back, she gazed up at the ceiling, which seemed to be moving from side to side. Feeling nauseated, she quickly snapped her eyes shut again. *Where am I,* she thought. The seven tequila shots from the night before had completely clouded her memory. The only thing she knew for sure was that she felt disgusting. There was crust in the corners of her eyes and her tongue and lips were dry.

She couldn't wait to get to a toothbrush and a wash cloth. Figuring it was best she got up and pieced the last ten hours of her life together, McKinley reopened her eyes and pulled back the covers. To her shock and dismay she found that she was stark naked.

"What the hell?" she uttered, pulling the covers back over her.

Then out of nowhere she heard the sound of a loud snort and realized that she wasn't alone. Scrunching her forehead, McKinley gradually turned her head to the right and found a toned muscular back facing her. *Umm,* she thought as a still-sleeping Koran turned over and faced her. *Oh, my God, I slept with the guy from the restaurant.*

"Oh, my God," she groaned, running her hands down her face. "What were you thinking, McKinley," she whispered.

Out of nowhere, as if an alarm was set off inside of her, McKinley remembered her flight.

"Shit," she shrieked, jumping out of the bed.

Yes, she was mortified by her drunken rendezvous with the stranger, but she'd deal with that later. There was no way on God's green earth that she was missing her flight. She couldn't; after that day she had no place to stay. Quietly, McKinley searched the hotel room for her things. She and Koran's clothes and shoes were thrown about, all over the room.

Locating her bra, which was by the door, she bent over to pick it up, but a wave of dizziness swarmed her head. *I will never drink tequila again,* she swore, standing up straight. With as much speed as she could muster, McKinley whizzed around the room, gathering and putting on her things. Minutes later, she was fully dressed and ready to go. With her hand on the knob, she glanced over her shoulder at Koran who was still asleep.

She wondered if she should at least say good-bye. But what kind of good-bye would it be? *Hey, it was nice having sex with you. I'll see you later* or *glad we fucked; too bad we'll never see each other again.* Deciding that saying good-bye wasn't the best idea, McKinley stared at him a second more. The sight of his handsome face, lying there looking so peaceful brought back memories of Jamil. She knew that it was dumb, being as though Jamil was a lying, cheating whore, but she couldn't help but feel like she was betraying him.

Hell, the man had just died a couple of weeks before. Besides, sleeping with Koran had just been another mistake to add to her list of fuck-ups in life. Remembering her flight, McKinley shrugged her shoulders and opened the door, vowing that from that moment forward she would do everything in her power to get her life back on track.

XoXo

McKinley said a silent prayer to God, thanking Him for allowing her to make it to the airport in just enough time to board the plane. It had been a race against the clock, but she made it. Sitting in her seat, she turned her cell phone off and placed it inside her purse. Closing her eyes, she leaned her head back and turned it to the side facing the window. The hangover she was nursing was kicking her ass. She couldn't wait for the plane to take off, so she could ask a flight attendant for some aspirins. What McKinley didn't know was that in a few seconds her headache was about to take a turn from bad to worst.

"Excuse me," Koran said, easing his way down the aisle.

He'd barely made it to the airport. If it wasn't for his daughter calling him to say good morning he'd probably still be asleep. He just knew that when he woke up McKinley would still be by his side, but to his surprise she was already gone. He wondered had it all been a dream. Maybe he'd conjured the whole thing up in his head. All he knew for sure was that he had to get home to his baby girl.

Koran found his seat, which was in the very back of the plane. *Goddamnit, I got the aisle seat*, he thought. Koran hated the aisle seat. Flight attendants were always bumping into him and he couldn't see out the window good. Since he refused to check in luggage, Koran opened the overhead compartment and squeezed his bag inside. Dying to sit down and relax, he sat down next to the young lady who lucked up and got a window seat. As Koran adjusted himself in his seat his left elbow accidently nudged the woman.

"Sorry," he said as she turned and looked at him with disdain.

"You!" McKinley sat up surprised.

"Me?" Koran shot back.

"Yeah, you." McKinley rolled her neck. "What the hell are you doing here? Are you some kind of stalker or something?"

"Man, please, you wish." Koran waved her off. "I'm heading home to St. Louis."

"Okay, now this is too much. I'm heading home to St. Louis,

too. You sure you're not no hired hit man?" McKinley looked around nervously.

Maybe whoever killed Jamil was planning on killing her next.

"If I was would I tell you?" Koran shot sarcastically.

"This is some bullshit," McKinley said, outraged.

"You can say that again," Koran agreed.

"Everyone, please fasten your seatbelts Delta Airlines, flight sixty-eight, leaving Miami, Florida and heading to Atlanta, Georgia is preparing for takeoff. Please turn off all electronic devices."

"So, you're trying to tell me that none of this was planned?" McKinley said in a low tone while buckling her seat belt.

"That you didn't seek me out on purpose and that you didn't book a seat on the same flight as me on purpose? This is just all purely coincidental?" She eyed him skeptically.

"Yes," Koran replied annoyed.

"I don't care nothin' about you having an attitude. I'm tryin' to make sure you're not out to kill me."

"The question is, why are you so concerned with somebody tryin' to kill you?" Koran stared at her.

McKinley sat speechless. There was no way she was gonna tell him about Jamil.

"That's beside the point," she huffed. "Did somebody hire you to kill me or what?" she shouted, causing everyone on the plane to turn around.

"Will you shut the fuck up?" Koran clasped his hand over her mouth. "Everything's fine, she's just rehearsing for a play she's in, sorry," he assured the other passengers.

Once everyone was settled back into their seats, Koran released his hand from McKinley's mouth.

"I hope your hands are clean." She screwed up her face.

"Fuck all of that. Let me tell you something." Koran pulled her close to him and whispered into her ear. "If I wanted you dead you'd be dead by now, so you can stop wit' all that rah rah. Now sit yo' ass back and enjoy the fuckin' ride."

"Well, excuse me. You don't have to be rude," McKinley scoffed as the plane took off on the runway

McKinley gripped the arms of the seat tight. She hated flying. The thought of being that high up in the air with no safety net was terrifying. McKinley squeezed her eyes tight and repeated to herself "Oh, God! Oh, God! Oh, God! Oh, God! Oh, God!"

Koran glanced over at her and noticed her chanting. Because she was holding on to the seat so tight, her knuckles were stark white. Koran wanted to be a dick and ignore her whining, but every time he gazed at her thoughts of his late wife, Whitney, appeared. She hated to fly, too.

"Are you gon' be doin' this the whole flight?" he asked.

"Doing what?" McKinley opened her right eye.

"Whining."

"I'm not whining. I'm praying. Something you obviously know nothin' about," she snapped.

Koran ignored her comment and said, "Whatever you doing,

can you stop? It's gettin' on my nerves."

"Oh, my God, you are such a jerk. You've never met someone who's afraid of takeoff?" McKinley asked.

"At least they appreciated my help." He thought back to Whitney again.

"How are you helping me? By being an asshole?" McKinley quipped.

Koran ignored her sarcasm. "Just say thank you."

"Say thank you for what?" McKinley looked at him confused.

"Look." He pointed toward the window.

McKinley looked out the window and realized that they were no longer taking off, but in the air, surrounded by a sea of clouds.

"Now say thank you." Koran placed his head back, closed his eyes and smiled.

"I wish I would." McKinley rolled her eyes.

"That's cool. Don't ask me for help no more."

"I didn't in the first place." She folded her arms across her chest.

Thirty minutes later, after sitting in silence and trying their best to pretend that the other didn't exist, the sky had gone from blue to gray. A heavy thunderstorm had formed and was causing the plane to experience a lot of turbulence.

McKinley stopped a flight attendant as she made her way down the aisle. "What's happening?"

"It's just a little turbulence. Everything will be fine," the flight attendant assured with a smile, trying her best not to fall.

McKinley panicked. "Why is this happening to me?"

"Didn't you just hear what the flight attendant just said?" Koran asked. "Everything gon' be straight."

But as soon as the words came out of his mouth the plane shook violently, causing the yellow oxygen masks to fall from the ceiling.

"This is your captain speaking, ladies and gentlemen. I may have underestimated the storm just a tad bit. But I'm afraid we are being diverted to Jacksonville Airport, as Atlanta International Airport has been shut down. Once we land, the staff will be happy to book you onto connecting flights, in order to get you to your final destination."

"I told you." McKinley began to cry. "We're all going to die!" She screamed, "Jesus, take me now."

"I'd rather argue wit' you than to be with someone else."

Kanye West feat John Legend and Chris Rock "Blame Game"

The main terminal of Jacksonville Airport was filled with enraged and shaken-up passengers, trying to figure out how they were going to get to their destinations. Among the slew of people was McKinley. After sitting and waiting three hours for a seat on a plane, she bombarded her way through the crowd with her purse in hand. Although it had been said repeatedly that all flights were canceled due to inclement weather she was determined to find a way out of Hicksville USA and fast.

She questioned an elderly woman behind the service desk. "So are you telling me that there are absolutely no flights leaving out of here until tomorrow?

"Nope," the woman said, not even bothering to look up.

"None?" McKinley said in disbelief.

The woman looked up at her. "I believe that's what I said the first time."

"Well, see," McKinley looked at the woman's name tag, "Cricket, I have a huge problem with that, 'cause I need to get home today."

"So does everybody else, Prima Donna."

McKinley frowned at the woman and turned around pissed. She was even more upset to find that Koran was sitting right behind her and had overheard everything.

She screwed up her face. "What the hell are you laughing at?"

"Nothing." He chuckled.

"I swear this is some bullshit."

She didn't know how her life could get any worse. Her man,

who was really somebody else's man, was dead. She was broke, homeless and stranded in a city where it looked like the local Wal-Mart was the hippest place in town.

"Mr. McKnight, your car is ready," a Hertz representative said to Koran.

Koran stood up, gathered his things and walked over to the Hertz station to pick up his keys. McKinley watched him eagerly like a fat kid who was dying for the last piece of cake. Sure she'd been a bitch to him all morning, but there was no way she could allow him to leave without taking her with him.

"Koran," she called out.

Koran stopped mid-stride and smiled to himself. Before turning around, he erased the smile off of his face.

"What?" he asked with an attitude.

"I assume you're driving back to St. Louis?"

"You would assume right."

"Look, I know we've had our moments, but is there any way I could ride back with you?"

He shook his head. "I don't know about that."

"Why not? I promise I won't even bother you. Hell, I won't even talk to you if you don't want me to."

"Put that on something." Koran twisted his lips to the side, not believing her.

"I put that on everything," she lied.

"Cool, but I'ma need one more thing from you."

"What?" McKinley eyed him quizzically.

Koran stepped into her personal space. "A kiss."

"You out yo' damn mind," McKinley scoffed.

"A'ight, stay yo' ass here then." Koran began to walk away.

"Really?" she challenged.

"Yeah." Koran looked at her.

"This is not right." McKinley approached him.

"You either gon' do it or you ain't," Koran replied.

Knowing she had no other choice but to either put up or shut up, McKinley wrapped her arms around his neck and gave him the most sensuous kiss he'd ever had. Right there in the middle of the airport their lips and tongues intertwined.

"Are you happy now?" McKinley asked, stepping back.

"I mean, yeah. I just asked for a peck, you ain't have to put ya' tongue all in my mouth." Koran twisted up his face, pretending as if he hadn't enjoyed every second of it.

"Whatever. Can we go now?" McKinley rolled her eyes.

"Yeah, but if you get out of line one more time yo' ass is out."

She raised her right arm and saluted him. "I promise I'll behave. Scout's honor."

XoXo

Relived that she finally had a way home, McKinley walked through the revolving door and outside to the roaring, windy thunderstorm. McKinley dropped her head low and tried her best to conceal herself, but to no affect. The wind was so forceful that she couldn't even walk at a normal pace or stand straight. She tried calling out for Koran who was ahead of her, but every time she went to open her mouth a sea of water would choke her.

After what seemed like a five-mile walk they finally made it to the car, which was a bright yellow 2011 PT Cruiser. McKinley couldn't believe her eyes. This had to have been some kind of sick joke. No way was this the rental car. McKinley was so taken aback by the vehicle that she didn't even hear Koran calling out her name.

"McKinley," he shouted once again, holding onto to the hood of the trunk.

"Huh?" She blinked her eyes, coming back to reality.

"The door is open," he shouted.

Nodding her head, McKinley got inside the car with a bewildered expression on her face. Drenched, she slowly placed on her seatbelt while wondering was this all a bad dream. The car was so bright it made her head hurt.

"Whew." Koran sighed, wiping the drops of rain from his face.

McKinley looked at him. "This is a joke, right?"

"Is what a joke?" Koran asked perplexed.

"This car." She looked around.

"I know it's brighter than a muthafucka, but it's the only thing they had left. It was either this or a yellow Bug."

"I will be so glad when I see the *Welcome to Missouri* sign, so this trip from hell can be over with," McKinley replied.

"That's like the second thing you've said all day that I've agreed with." Koran started up the engine, only for it to cut off seconds later.

"Now what do you have to say, Big Mouth?" McKinley folded her arms across her chest.

"Didn't we agree, no talkin'?" Koran turned the key again.

This time the car cranked up right away without any problem.

"It ain't my fault you fell for that shit." McKinley giggled.

"Whatever. You just sit back and look pretty. I got this."

"Uh huh." McKinley pursed her lips, trying her best not to smile.

Koran was a cutie pie, but he was arrogant as hell. From the little that she could remember about their night of passion, his sex game wasn't too shabby either. But what could a one-night stand lead to? It wasn't like they were going to fall madly in love and ride off into the sunset and live happily ever after.

1. They barely knew each other.

2. He could be crazy.

3. He might have a hint of beat-a-bitch down in him.

4. He could very well already have a woman.

5. He could have fifty million kids spread around the United States.

6. He could be crazy!

Besides that, McKinley was still mourning the death of Jamil. The wounds of his death and betrayal hadn't even begun to heal. Plus, what honestly did she have to offer a dog, let alone a fine, strong, cocky-ass man like Koran? She needed to get herself in order before she could jump into anything. Needing to hear something inspirational, McKinley leaned forward and turned the radio station from the FM Hip Hop and R&B station Koran was playing to an AM gospel station.

"Another's Day Journey" by Lashuan Pace was playing. McKinley gazed out of the window and tapped her foot while singing along.

"I got my health and strength y'all—"

Koran switched the station back to the FM side.

McKinley shot him a look that could kill and switched it back to AM.

"A lil Jesus never hurt nobody," she said.

"And neither did a lil JayZ." Koran pushed her hand away and turned the knob once more.

Determined to beat him at his own game, McKinley pinched him in the arm and switched the knob back to Lashuan Pace.

"Oww, that shit hurt.' Koran yanked his arm up and down then quickly turned the station.

"OOOOOOOOOH!" McKinley mockingly groaned, forcefully turning the knob back, but this time causing it break off.

"Look at what you did!" She held the knob up. "Now neither of us can listen to the radio."

Koran pulled over to the side of the road. "Get out!"

"What?" McKinley looked at him like he was crazy.

"Get out!"

"You're kidding me?"

"Does it look like I'm playin' wit' you? Get out!" Koran reached over her and opened the passenger side door.

"I can't get out and walk. I have on Chanel heels." She pouted.

"Oh, yes you can, and you will." Koran unbuckled her seatbelt.

"But I'm sorry." McKinley poked out her bottom lip.

"No, you're not."

"Yes, I am." McKinley smiled and nodded her head simultaneously.

"Sorry for what?" Koran inquired.

"I'm sorry I broke the knob."

"What else?"
McKinley held her head down and whispered, "I'm sorry I turned the station without asking."

"You're missing something."

"I'm sorry I spoke out loud." She rolled her eyes.

"Thank you. That's better. Now close your door," Koran ordered while making his way back onto the road.

Part Three

"No one has to know what you are feeling, no one but me and you."

Alicia Keys
"Diary"

"No, no!" McKinley shook her from side to side while asleep. "No, Jamil! Jamil!" she screamed, jumping out her sleep, scaring Koran half to death.

"Oh, my God!" She inhaled and exhaled.

"What the fuck is wrong wit' you?" Koran asked, trying his best to stay focused on the road.

"Nothin'." McKinley panted, holding her chest.

"I don't know about you, but to me that was something."

"I said it was nothin'," McKinley insisted, wiping her face with her hands.

"Then who is Jamil?" Koran quizzed.

McKinley snapped her neck to the side and looked at him.

"What did you just say?"

"I said who is Jamil?" Koran replied, bluntly.

"Nobody." McKinley leaned back.

"He must be somebody, you over there dreaming about him," Koran replied back.

"Will you mind yo' damn business? He's nobody. Now can you stop at the next exit? I have to pee or is that up for discussion too?"

By the expression on her face, Koran could tell that he'd overstepped his boundaries. Instead of putting her in her place for talkin' slick, Koran did as he was asked and got off the highway. A Shell station was down the road, so he stopped there. He wasn't even parked well at a pump before McKinley jumped out and slammed the door behind her. Inside the restroom, McKinley turned on the faucet and let the cool water run over her hands. Relishing the sensation, she splashed the soothing water onto her face.

After grabbing a paper towel and drying her face off, McKinley gazed at herself in the mirror. Ever since Jamil died she'd had trouble sleeping. Most nights she stayed awake as long as she could in fear of the nightmares she was sure to have. McKinley just wanted her life to get back to normal. But what about her life was normal? She was taking a road trip home with a complete stranger whom she'd had a one-night stand with the night before.

Thinking of Koran made McKinley feel horrible. He was only trying to figure out what was wrong with her and she'd completely gone off on him. Not liking what she saw staring back at her in the mirror, McKinley walked out of the restroom. Koran stood at the side of the car, pumping gas, when he noticed every time he looked at her the hairs on his arm stood up. She was petite compared to Whitney, but her face and dimples were the exact same. She seemed to have been dropped down from heaven. He knew McKinley probably thought he was weird for randomly staring at her all the time, but he couldn't take his eyes off of her.

The only way he could tell McKinley and Whitney apart was by their personalities. Whitney was far more gentle and soft-spoken. Not to say she didn't know how to get rowdy when necessary. Koran missed his wife terribly. Thoughts of her caused his heart to ache. He'd give anything to have her back in his arms again and to be there to see their daughter grow.

But no matter how much he wished and prayed, his prayers weren't going to come true. Tank filled, Koran got back into the car and started the engine. On the road again, he and McKinley sat quietly. Unable to bear the silence, McKinley began to talk.

"I'm sorry for snapping on you like that."

"It's cool."

"No, it's not." She looked down at her hands. Tears were starting to slowly form in her eyes. "My life is a mess." McKinley began to cry.

Koran looked over at her.

"You, a'ight?" he asked, concerned.

"No." She wiped her eyes. "A couple of weeks ago my fiancé was killed." "Damn, for real? That's fucked up," Koran said sincerely.

"Tell me about it," McKinley agreed. "I didn't even get to go to the funeral."

"Why?"

"'Cause he was married." McKinley cried even harder.

"What?" Koran said, shocked.

"After he died I found out that he'd been living a double life. The whole three years we were together he had a whole wife, kids and a whole nother chick on the side and my dumbass didn't even know it. I mean, how gullible could I possibly be? I had no clue."

"That's some deep shit," Koran said, overwhelmed by her confession.

"Since he passed my whole life has been turned upside down. All I knew was him. He was my everything. My whole life was centered around him."

"Well, see, that's where you fucked up."

"What?" She blew her nose on a napkin.

"I don't give a fuck how much you love a man; never make him your whole world. That's where y'all females fuck up."

"Thanks for making me feel even worse." McKinley chuckled.

"My bad. I wasn't tryin' to be mean or nothin'. I'm just statin' facts." Koran shrugged.

"If you say so."

"Nah, for real. I'm sorry for your loss. It's a fucked-up feeling losing someone you love. No matter what the circumstances are," Koran said somberly.

"I know that shit gotta hurt," he continued.

"Like hell," she agreed.

"So that's why you were in tears yesterday?"

"How did you know I'd been cryin'?" McKinley asked, surprised.

"'Cause your eyes were red and you looked like you'd lost your favorite Chanel bag or something," Koran teased.

"You stupid." McKinley laughed.

"I'm serious. I was like 'Damn, let me go give this girl a hug before she have to be put on suicide watch'," he teased.

"I did look pitiful, didn't I?" McKinley sniffled.

"You said it. I didn't." Koran chuckled.

"It's cool. I know I did."

"On the real though," Koran said, "I understand that you're

hurting now and the pain will last for a while, but eventually things will get better. One day you're going to wake up and it's not going to hurt as bad. The pain will go from a throbbing sensation to just a little sting."

"How do you know so much about mourning someone's death?"

"My mother died of an overdose when I was a teenager."

"Wow. I'm sorry," McKinley said, flabbergasted.

"It's all good," he assured.

"Death is never good. You can say how you really feel around me."

"I mean, I felt abandoned, but I did what I had to do to survive."

"Like what?"

"I sold dope, but a good friend of mine helped me realize that wasn't the route to go, so I stopped."

"What do you do now?"

"I own a couple of businesses back home."

"That's good. Most dudes don't ever stop. Case and point, my fiancé."

"Yeah, well, I had reasons outside of my control that got me out the game." Koran thought back to Whitney's illness and the birth of his daughter.

"Really? What?"
"Ay, you hungry?" Koran asked, changing the subject.

"Always." McKinley grinned.

"Let's grab something to eat. All of this talkin' has made me hungry."

"Okay." She smiled, genuinely enjoying his company.

"I'm here as long as you
need me"

Brandy
"All In Me"

For the next two hours McKinley and Koran laughed and talked about everything from childhood memories, favorite restaurants to their top five MC's. On the surface, things were cool, but underlying emotions from the night before and untold details from their lives stayed stuck on pause in their throat.

"How can you not respect Kanye?" Koran asked, amped.

"Ever since I saw him rock a leopard-print shirt his ass been a lil suspect to me. I'm tellin' you, that negro got *How you doing?* written all over him." McKinley flicked her wrist.

"Get the fuck outta here." Koran laughed, yawning. "So what did you do for a living back in Miami?"

"Umm," McKinley stammered.

She couldn't just come out and say nothing. It would make her look like a bird.

"I was a personal shopper," she lied.

"That's what's up." Koran nodded his head.

"Yo, I'm gettin' tired. I think we need to get a room for the night and start fresh in the morning." He looked over at her. "I saw a sign for a Marriot hotel a couple of miles back, so it should be coming up soon."

McKinley panicked. "I'll drive. I'm not tired."

If she had to tell Koran that she was broke on top of everything she'd revealed she'd die of embarrassment.

"Please, you've been over there yawning yo' ass off. Ain't no way in hell I'ma let you behind this wheel," he declared.

"I promise you, I'm good," McKinley protested.

"Nah, we both need to rest. Plus, I could use a bath, so I know you got to be dying for one, too."

"What you tryin' to say?" McKinley cocked her head back.

"Fall back," Koran laughed, getting off the highway. "I ain't tryin' to say nothin'. I'm sayin' you need to wash yo' ass," he joked.

McKinley ignored his sarcasm. "But what if it's a nasty Marriot with dingy carpeting and a moldy smell?"

"Does this look like a dingy Marriot to you?" Koran asked, pulling into the parking lot.

McKinley looked up at the building. Koran was right. It was a nice hotel. The Marriot hotel in Knoxville, Tennessee was on a hilltop overlooking the Tennessee River. *Dammit*, McKinley thought. She had to find a way out of this somehow. In a last ditch effort to change Koran's mind she said, "I really feel uneasy about this. Something in my spirit is just sayin' this ain't right."

"Chill out. Everything's going to be fine. From the looks of it this has to be at least a four-star hotel. Now come on." Koran got out of the car and popped the trunk.

With only one more option left McKinley grabbed her purse from the back seat of the car and got out as well. As Koran strolled into the hotel McKinley lagged behind him slowly. At the service desk Koran paid for his room.

"Have a wonderful night, sir." The front desk clerk smiled.

"You, too." Koran smiled back, taking his key.

"You know what?" McKinley slapped her hand against her forehead. "I think I left something in the car. Let me get the keys, so I can run back and go get it."

"Here." Koran tossed her the keys. "You want me to wait on you?"

"No, go ahead up to your room. I'll be fine," she assured as the elevator doors opened.

"A'ight." Koran turned and hopped inside.

As the doors to the elevator closed McKinley let out a sigh of relief. Swiftly, she walked back to the car, got in and locked the doors. For the first time that day she'd dodged a bullet successfully. She could've come out and told him the truth, but the truth was that McKinley was ashamed. She was ashamed that she'd allowed herself to be put in this position. For the last three years of her life she'd enjoyed the perks of dating a rich man, only to be left with nothing but designer tags.

The only sort of achievement she'd made in life thus far was mastering the art of a sample sale. Her pride was just too strong to let Koran know that she was penniless. She respected him and wanted him to respect her, too. Her life was already in shambles. The last thing she needed was Koran looking down at her.

"McKinley!" Koran tapped on the passenger side window, causing her to jump.

"Huh?" She stared up at him.

"What are you doing?"

"Umm," she tried to think of a lie. "I was lookin' for my lipstick." She smiled.

"Open the door," Koran insisted.

McKinley unlocked the door, knowing she'd been caught.

"Now are you gon' tell me the truth or do I have to pry it out of you?"

McKinley gazed off to the side. She felt like a little kid who'd been caught with her hand in the cookie jar.

"I don't have any money," she finally said.

"You're broke?" Koran asked, surprised.

"Yeah, like broke, broke. After Jamil died the Feds froze all of my accounts. All I have is the money in my pocket, which is nothing but twenty dollars. My mother and best friend had to pay for my airline ticket home." Her lips trembled.

"Who are you?" Koran eyed her suspiciously. "I mean, is your name even McKinley?"

"See, this is why I didn't wanna tell you." McKinley tried to close the door, but Koran stopped her by pulling it back open.

"What?" she whined.

"What do you really think you're doing?"

"I don't know."

"Look, even though you're a walkin', talkin' Lifetime movie, you can sleep in my room."

She shook her head. "You don't have to do that."

"I know I don't." He winked his eye.

After riding the elevator up to the third floor, Koran and McKinley entered room 315. McKinley was pleasantly surprised at how clean and chic the room was. On the bed there was a brand-new down comforter and fluffy white pillows. Instead of using hotel bath soaps, they used Bath and Body Works products. Worn out from the day, McKinley kicked off her heels. Her feet were killing her. Unbeknownst to McKinley, while she stretched her toes, Koran had started to strip down.

"Oh, my God, you were right. I didn't even realize until now how tired I was." She yawned. "I just thought about it though. I don't have anything to put on."

"Here, you can wear one of my T-shirts." Koran threw one at her.

McKinley turned around to catch it and noticed that Koran had nothing on but a pair of boxer briefs.

"What the hell?" she yelled.

"What's wrong wit' you?" He rummaged through his suitcase for something to sleep in.

"Umm, dude, you couldn't go in the bathroom and change?" McKinley shielded her eyes with her hand.

She prayed to God he couldn't see how red her face was.

"It ain't like you ain't never seen me naked before." Koran took off his underwear and walked past her.

McKinley couldn't risk taking a peek. Koran's ass was so firm you could bounce a quarter off of it. McKinley wasn't even aware how hard she was staring at him until he spun around unexpectedly. His ten-inch dick was staring her smack dab in the face. His dick was surely something she'd forgotten during their drunken tryst.

How she could've erased that from her memory was beyond her, because his dick was a mouthwatering sight to see. It was long and thick and the tip reminded her of a tootsie roll Blow Pop that she wanted to suck all of the flavor out of.

"McKinley!" Koran shouted, getting her attention.

"Huh?" She blinked her eyes.

"You mind ordering some room service?" Koran asked, knowing damn well his body was causing her to go into convulsions.

Once the order was placed McKinley retrieved her cell phone and called her mother to let her know she was okay. By the time she ended the call, Koran was coming out of the bathroom. McKinley tried to act like he didn't have any effect on her as she grabbed her things and walked past him, but her eyes kept gravitating to the bulge in his underwear. The cup could barely hold his dick, it was so big.

Needing to get herself together, McKinley scurried into the bathroom and closed the door behind her. With her back against the door, she wondered would she be able to stay in the same room with Koran without taking every inch of his manhood in her mouth. *I mean, ain't nothin' wrong wit a lil bump and grind,* she thought. Deciding it was best she take a cold shower, McKinley turned on the water and got naked.

The cold water was freezing, but it helped get her mind in order. She couldn't continue to let Koran take her off her game. She had to stay focused on the task at hand, which was getting home in one piece and figuring out her life from then on. Fresh and clean, McKinley stepped out of the shower. Minutes later she dried off, lathered on lotion and slipped on the T-shirt Koran had given her.

The shirt barely covered her ass cheeks, but it would have to do because she had no other options. It was, however, the first time McKinley wished she wore panties. Gathering her clothes, she opened the door. The first thing she noticed was Koran sitting on the edge of the bed, eating the juiciest burger she'd ever seen. Upon sight, her stomach instantly growled. She was mortified. The sound was so loud that even Koran heard it.

"Did you just fart?" He scrunched up his forehead, disgusted.

"No. That was my stomach." Her cheeks turned beet red.

"Yeah, okay." Koran scrunched up his face and continued chewing. "Your food is over there on the table." He gestured with his head.

"Thanks," McKinley replied, folding her clothes as quickly as possible.

The smell of the burger was driving her mad. McKinley didn't even bother to sit down. She simply popped off the lid and devoured the bacon cheeseburger right there on the spot. A bit of juice from the meat trickled down her chin, but she didn't care. Her stomach was saying, "Feed me, bitch." McKinley was eating so fast that Koran stopped eating his food and sat back and watched her in awe.

Full and exhausted from the long day they'd endured; McKinley and Koran slipped underneath the covers and lay down. Both made sure to lie as far away from the other as possible. Although being in such close proximity to each other was making both of their temperatures rise. Koran lay on his back, gazing up at the ceiling. He'd never once in his life lay beside a woman in bed and not touch her.

McKinley was so close to him that he could reach out and touch her, but he didn't want to invade her personnel space. Instead of acting on impulse, Koran swung his legs out of the bed and sat up. His muscular back faced McKinley as he glided his hands over his head and down his face. McKinley watched him in awe. So many erotic thoughts bombarded her mind, she couldn't think straight.

With every blink of the eye and movement of her body, she yearned for him. All she could imagine was him lying on top of her and caressing her thighs. Her body needed him in the worst way. Nervous as hell, McKinley crawled over to his side of the bed and wrapped her arms around his neck.

"What you doing, man?" Koran asked, relishing the feel of her tongue on his earlobe.

"Exactly what you want me to do." McKinley placed a trail of light kisses from his ear to his cheek.

"You sure you wanna do this?"

"Mmm hmm." McKinley ran her hand down his chest.

She then strategically slipped her head inside his boxers and began massaging his rock-hard dick. Turned on to the fullest, Koran turned his face to the side and stared at her. McKinley was beautiful and if he made love to her he wasn't going to hold anything back. Figuring they were two consenting adults who knew exactly what they were getting themselves into, he gently cupped McKinley's face with his hands and kissed her lips. As their tongues intertwined, McKinley found herself drowning with every touch of his hand. Koran felt the same exact way. Laying on top of her, he swiftly ran his hand up her shirt and toyed with her nipples.

With every stroke of his fingers, McKinley's temperature rose. Koran stared into her big brown eyes. McKinley was beautiful. Her voluptuous physique melted his heart. Koran couldn't wait to enter her wet slit again. She was so warm, he could stay there forever. Knowing exactly what was on his mind, McKinley parted her legs.

She had to have him. The need for him to be inside of her grew with each second. All she could think about were his deep kisses and his strong hands massaging her breasts while he grinded in and out of her at a feverish pace. Always one to please, Koran slipped his manhood into her warm hole. The feeling was sensational.

McKinley held onto his back and willed herself not to come. She wanted this moment to last forever. Being with Koran sexually was unlike anything she'd ever experienced before. He took his time with her. He made sure she felt every stroke, every bite, ever lick of his tongue. That night, underneath the light of the pale moon, their bodies twisted against each other in slow ecstasy. Flesh to flesh, they consumed one another until both their desires were met and neither could go anymore.

"She can't see in me what I see in her."

Wale feat Marsha Ambrosius
"Diary"

"You ready?" Koran asked the next morning.

"Yep." McKinley looked at him then turned her head.

The first time they'd slept together both were in a drunken stupor. The next morning; memories of each touch, kiss and thrust was clouded. But last night they both were fully aware. Their bodies had become one in the most erotic way. Now, as they resumed their road trip home, both wondered had they made the right decision by taking it there, because now there was no turning back.

They couldn't blame their actions on the alcohol. Every moan, whimper and scream had come from the most sacred place inside their hearts. For a while they both rode in silence, too afraid to speak what was on their minds. Instead of talking, Koran and McKinley took in the scenic view. Nothing but acres of grass filled with corn and sugar cane surrounded them. Inside the car, Koran and McKinley began to hear a popping sound come from the engine.

"Oh, my God! What is that?" McKinley sat up, frightened.

"The engine." Koran rode along the rode cautiously.

"Why is it making that noise?" McKinley's voice shook slightly.

"Like I know."

McKinley panicked. "Please tell me that's not smoke."

"Where?" Koran said, alarmed.

McKinley pointed. "The hood!"

"Fuck!" Koran hit the steering wheel, heated.

"Lord, help me! We're gettin' ready to die. And I didn't even get to see Beyonce live in concert," McKinley screeched.

Koran tried his best to continue down the road, but sputtering noises, loud pops that sounded like gunshots, and smoke coming from the engine made him realize he had no choice but to stop.

"Why are you pulling over?"

"'Cause I think the transmission's gone out." Koran turned off the engine and got out.

"Oh, my God! You have got to be fuckin' kidding me." McKinley placed her head back against the headrest and closed her eyes.

"This cannot be happening to me."

"Fuck!" Koran slammed the hood shut.

"C'mon, man, we gon' have to walk." He took the keys out of the ignition.

McKinley looked at him like he was crazy. "Excuse you? These shoes ain't made for walkin'."

"Well, I don't know what to tell you. I'm gettin' ready to walk until I find something." Koran took his luggage out of the trunk.

"We're in the middle of nowhere. Do you know how long that could be?" McKinley yelled out of the window.

"I don't care. I'm not staying here," Koran yelled over his shoulder as he walked with his baggage in tow.

"Well, I'm not walkin' no damn where." McKinley folded her arms across her chest. "What the hell I look like?"

But as McKinley looked around at the acres of land and thought about what could possibly be lurking around in it she became overwhelmingly scared. Realizing that she had no other choice but to walk, she grabbed her purse and got out of the car.

"Wait on me!" She jogged toward Koran.

"I thought you would come to your senses," he teased.

She pushed him in the arm. "Shut up."

Two hours into their hike, McKinley's feet were on fire. Her feet hurt so bad, she walked with a limp. She was almost sure she had a blister or two on her feet as well. Koran felt bad for her. He would've gladly picked her up and carried her, but he had his luggage to pull.

"I can't do this much longer," McKinley whined as tears poured from her eyes.

"I know, baby." Koran stopped walking and helped her ease her way down to the ground to sit.

McKinley's heart skipped a beat. She hadn't expected for Koran to call her baby.

"What are we gonna do?" She tried her best not to blush.

"I think I see something up the road. Look, you just stay here and rest and watch my bags. I'll be back as soon as I can."

"Uh ah." McKinley's eyes grew wide. "You ain't gon' leave me out here in the wilderness for some crazy ass to come out of the woodworks and come kill me. No, no. I'll walk some more if I have to."

"No, you won't and you can't. I promise I'll be back in less than an hour. I'ma run there and back."

McKinley inhaled deeply. After dealing with Jamil, and his unreliability, she had a hard time trusting Koran's word, but something in his eyes told her that he was telling the truth.

"Okay, but hurry back."

"I will." Koran kissed her on the forehead before running off.

McKinley watched Koran until his back faded. Alone and a little afraid, she took off her heels and massaged her red, aching and swollen feet. Every now and then she'd hear something rattle in the wind that caused her to jump. But for the most part, McKinley was able to keep her cool. That was until she saw something big, brown and furry traipsing across the field.

"Oh, my God! It's Big Foot." She got up off the ground to get a better view of the huge creature.

"Yeah, that's most definitely Big Foot," she panicked.

"I see now I'ma have to fuck Big Foot up." She picked up her heel, ready to strike.

But it wasn't Big Foot. McKinley's fear and wild imagination had gotten the best of her. What she thought was Big Foot was really only a wolf. The wolf, however, was now only a few feet away from her. This was it. McKinley was scared shitless, but she wasn't about to go down without a fight. Just as the wolf was nearing, Koran came zooming down the road in a pick-up truck driven by an older white man. Thankfully, the speed and un-expectancy of the truck scared the wolf away.

"Hallelujah, thank you, Jesus!" McKinley rushed over into Koran's arms. "Did you see it?" she asked terrified.

"See what?" He held her close.

McKinley pointed. "The half-man, half-wolf. It was just over there in the field."

Koran hung his head and smiled.

"Yo, I think you been out in the sun too long."

"I'm not crazy. One of the wolves from *Twilight* was about to make me his dinner."

"Aww shucks, that wasn't nothin' but an ole stray dog," the older white gentleman said.

"Who the hell is that?" McKinley whispered to Koran.

"McKinley, this kind man is Bobby Joe. He and his lovely wife, Jodeen, own the Quickie Mart down the road, and would you believe that on top of the Quickie Mart is a room?" Koran said, excited.

"That's wonderful," McKinley responded dryly.

"Well, grab your things and let's get a move on," Bobby Joe said. "*Nash Bridges* is about to come on."

"You ain't got to tell me twice." McKinley scurried and grabbed her things and got into the truck.

Koran threw his bags in the back of the truck and hopped into the front seat next to McKinley. Bobby Joe then started up the engine and they all rode down the street, making small talk.

"So how long you two lovebirds been married?" Bobby Joe questioned.

"Uh we're not—" McKinley uttered.

Koran cut her off. "Almost a year."

"Newlyweds, huh? Oh, I remember those days. Me and the missus have been married for over thirty years," Bobby Joe said proudly.

"Really?" McKinley looked over at Koran with an expression on her face that said, "When the hell did we get married?"

"Just play along," he mouthed.

"Here we are. Home sweet home." Bobby Joe pulled in front of the store.

"Koran, here are the keys. You and the missus can let yourselves in around the back. If you need anything, just come into the store and holler. If you need anything after store hours our farmhouse is right down the road, next to the bait shop."

"Thank you very much, Bobby Joe." Koran shook his hand.

"Yeah, thank you, Bobby Joe." McKinley smiled.

Koran used the key and unlocked the door to the room. It was just like he'd imagined it to be, small and quaint. Only the basics were in the room. There was a queen- sized bed, a nightstand with a rotary phone on top, a dresser and an old television with an antenna.

"Now why are we married again?" McKinley asked, sitting on the edge of the bed.

"Bobby Joe and his wife only rent out the room to married couples, so I told him what he wanted to hear, so we could have a place to stay tonight."

"Well, in that case, hubby, can I use your phone, 'cause my

battery went out?" McKinley batted her eyes.

"Yeah, here." Jamil handed her his phone. "I'm getting ready to get in the shower."

"Can I join you?" McKinley arched her eyebrow.

"I don't play that teasing shit. If you gon' do something just do it."

"I just might." McKinley winked her eye.

"Yeah, a'ight, we'll see." Koran dug into his bag and pulled out a fresh pair of underwear and clothes before heading into the shower.

McKinley called her mother.

Her mother answered on the first ring. "Hello?"

"Hi, Ma."

"McKinley, where are you?" Her mother's voice rose. "I've been callin' your phone all morning."

"I'm in Tennessee. The transmission went out."

"So when will you be home now?" her mother questioned.

"I guess in the next day or so. We're going to take the train now," McKinley explained.

"Where are y'all staying?"

"Koran rented us out a room."

"Okay, well call me tonight before you go to bed, so I can make sure you're all right."

"I will," McKinley assured as someone clicked onto the line. "Mama, I gotta click over. I'll call you later. Hello?"

"Hello?" a little girl said back.

"Hello? McKinley said again.

"Hello?"

"Hello?" McKinley said once more, taken aback.

"Helloooooo?" the little girl sang.

"Okay, who is this?" McKinley asked with an attitude.

"Harlow. Is my daddy there?"

"Your *daddy?*" McKinley said, taken aback.

"Yeah."

"Harlow, who is that?" a woman in the background asked.

"I don't know. I'm just lookin' for my daddy."

"Hand me the phone," the woman said.

Remembering what had happened with Jamil, McKinley didn't even bother speaking to the woman. Instead, she quickly hung up. It was like life was repeating itself all over again. She'd fallen once more for a man who led a secret life. Her life couldn't get any worse. She felt like a complete and utter fool. Tears flooded her eyes. McKinley swallowed hard. She was so caught up in her emotions that she hadn't even realized that the shower had stopped running and Koran had stepped back into the room.

"I guess you must've changed your mind?" he said, securing the towel around his waist.

"Fuck you!" she spat, throwing the phone at his chest.

"What the fuck is wrong wit' you?" Koran caught the phone mid-air.

"You!" she shrieked. "The damn broke-down plane. The fucked-up car, this dump." She swung her arms in the air. "Jamil's two-faced ass, that's what's wrong," McKinley snapped, picking up her shoes and purse.

"Where you going?" Koran asked, still perplexed.

"Anywhere but here," McKinley shouted, slamming the door behind her.

Unaware of where her sudden change in demeanor came from, Koran threw on his clothes and followed her. He found her sitting outside on the steps in the back of the building.

Koran sat down next to her. "What the hell is your problem?"

"Why didn't you tell me you were married?" McKinley sniffled.

"What are you talkin' about?" he questioned, confused.

"While I was on the phone with my mother your end clicked and I answered it." McKinley took a much-needed breath. "And some lil girl was on the line, then your wife got on the phone. And all I could think about was what happened with me and Jamil and I just felt so stupid. Like, how could I have not learned my lesson the first time." She sobbed. "You're way too fine to be single."

"First of all, I'm not married." Koran chuckled. "I mean, I am, but I'm not."

"Huh?" McKinley gazed up at him, perplexed.

"That must've been my daughter's nanny who got on the phone."

"So you *do* have a kid?" McKinley's heart dropped down to her knees.

"Yeah. I do." Koran nodded his head.

"Why didn't you tell me?"

"'Cause I didn't know you that well and I didn't feel like I had to," he stated matter of factly. "Real talk, ever since my daughter was born it's been just me and her. Her mother, my wife, Whitney, died after giving birth to her. She had cancer." Koran's voice trailed off.

"Koran, I am so sorry."

"It's cool."

"No, it's not. I am such an idiot." McKinley slapped her hand against her forehead. "Will you please forgive me?"

"You're forgiven, crybaby." Koran hugged her around her neck.

"But what I wanna know is where did you really think you were going?" He laughed.

"I don't know." She laughed, too.

"You crazy, but look, come with me." Koran stood up and wiped off the back of his pants.

"Where are we going?" McKinley asked, confused.

"Just come with me." He extended his hand.

"Have you forgotten that my feet are all swole?" McKinley extended her legs.

"Just come on." Koran pulled her up and drug her around to the front of the store.

Koran pulled the store's door open. The Quickie Mart was one of those stores that sold some of everything. They carried tires, fabric, bread, clothes, tools, you name it and you could find it.

"So this is your wife?" Jodeen smiled, coming from behind the counter.

Jodeen was a dead ringer for Paula Deen. Her hair was a sparkling silver shade, just like hers, and her baby-blue eyes lit up like the sky.

"She's even prettier then you described." Jodeen smiled at McKinley, cheerfully.

"Thank you." McKinley beamed.

"What can I do for you?" Jodeen spoke with a country twang.

"My wife lost her luggage," Koran began to explain.

"Poor dear." Jodeen clasped her hands together.

"So we need to pick up a few things for her to wear," Koran continued.

"You say what now?" McKinley cocked her head back.

"I have the perfect outfit." Jodeen cheerfully rushed over to the clothing section, which consisted of Dickies and John Deer.

"Everything in here is one-hundred-percent polyester," McKinley whispered. "If I'm even near polyester my skin breaks out."

"I'm tired of seeing you in this outfit, so you gon' have to do something," Koran declared.

"Here we are." Jodeen held up a pair of Dickies overalls. "Isn't it lovely?"

"Oh, it's special, all right." McKinley's upper lip curled.

"She'll take it," Koran chimed in.

"Whenever I'm alone
with you, you make me feel
like I am whole again."

Adele
"Lovesong"

The rest of the day, McKinley and Koran enjoyed each other's presence while lying in bed. They talked, slept and even made love again, but when the sun began to fall and their stomachs began to growl they knew it was time to get up. The bar across the street was the quickest place to get to on foot, so they headed over. Trudy's Place was like something out of a movie.

Everything from the tables to the jukebox was made of wood. On the walls were deer heads and old John Wayne posters. Outside of themselves only three other black people were in the spot, but Koran and McKinley didn't care. They were on a mission to eat and have a good time. The next morning they would be boarding a train back to St. Louis.

While waiting on Koran to return with their beer and wings, McKinley scratched her arms and legs profusely. She absolutely detested the wifebeater, overalls and tan- colored Timberland boots she wore. The rough and cheap fabric was driving her nuts. Other than that, she was having a wonderful time.

"Here you go, pretty girl." Koran sat her mug of beer down before her.

"Thank you. Ooh, these wings look yummy." McKinley rubbed her hands together, excited.

"Right, I'm hungrier than a muthafucka." Koran took a seat across from her.

"Yo, I swear to God I feel like I'm in the *Twilight Zone*." McKinley looked around the bar in awe. "I've only seen people like this on the *Simple Life* and *Toddlers and Tiaras*."

Koran cracked up laughing. "I know you got some family from the south. Every black person does," he said.

"Yeah, but this shit right here is a whole nother ballgame."

McKinley laughed, causing Koran to laugh, too.

"You know you look kinda cute in them bibs. You might need to come on up outta them when we get back to the room." He winked his eye.

"Oh, really, and what's gon' happen when I take'em off?"

"I'ma do what Lloyd said and lay it down."

"You so wack." McKinley laughed with glee.

Once they were done eating, McKinley and Koran played a game of pool and darts. McKinley wasn't very good at either, but Koran took the time to show her different techniques. Then the music slowed down and couples hit the dance floor.

"You wanna dance?" he asked, putting down the darts.

"Seriously?" McKinley eyed him quizzically.

"Why not?" He extended his hand.

McKinley placed her hand in his and followed him onto the dance floor. As their bodies became one, the twinkling lights around the room seemed to only shine on them. Hand in hand and chest to chest, they slow danced to "Lovesong" by British sensation Adele. The strum from the guitar transported McKinley and Koran to another realm in time.

No one else but them existed. To be in each other's arms felt right. It was like they belonged with one another. Koran rested his cheek on top of McKinley's head. Never in life did he think he'd ever feel this way again. Whitney had been the only woman for him. He never imagined he'd find someone who'd capture his heart the way she did.

McKinley, however, made him want to love again, being with her made him feel whole again. Her smile made him smile. For her, he'd put her hurt on his shoulders. Koran dreaded the fact that their journey was about to end. He wanted to stay with her forever.

McKinley pressed her face against Koran's chest, feeling the exact same way. For the last three years she'd had it all wrong. This was what love was supposed to feel like. It was uncomplicated and magical. A real man didn't put you in harm's way. He shielded you from pain. McKinley felt like she was floating on air.

She hadn't laughed and smiled this much in years. Koran brought out the best in her. She wanted to fix everything broken in him. He'd rescued her and she wanted to do the same. Koran placed his index finger underneath McKinley's chin and lifted her head up. She gazed up at him with tears in her eyes. After so much negativity, she'd found solace in something good.

Koran examined her face when suddenly a tear fell from her eyes and landed on his heart. After that he knew he couldn't be without her. McKinley stood on her tiptoes and kissed his lips. The bond they'd created was unbreakable. Some would even say bulletproof, but like all good things in life, what they shared had to come to an end.

XoXo

The rapid speed and constant rattling from the train jolted McKinley from side to side. For hours she'd tried to fall asleep, but the thoughts that raced through her head kept her awake. The closer she and Koran got to St. Louis, the more her mind filled with thoughts of dread. Over the last few days the unexpected had happened.

She hadn't seen it coming, but it felt right. She'd fallen in love. With Koran, everything was different, but in a good way. From the day they'd met he'd shown her more than Jamil had in the three years they'd been together. He made her feel like she mattered. He was generous and kind. He never left her out in the cold and most importantly his word was his bond. When he said he was going to do something he did it, unlike Jamil.

Koran laughed at her sarcasm and silliness. He didn't put her down or bail every time she did something he didn't like or agree with. When she was down he did whatever he could to lift her spirits. McKinley gazed over at him. Koran's head dangled to the side. He was asleep and snoring lightly. McKinley wanted to snuggle against him, but she didn't want to bother him.

Suddenly, Koran's eyes fluttered open and he looked over at her. McKinley grinned. She was slightly embarrassed that he'd caught her staring at him while he was asleep. She prayed to God he didn't think she was a creep.

"What you lookin' at, lil lady?" He yawned.

"Nothin'," she lied.

"Come here." Koran wrapped his arm around her neck and pulled her close.

McKinley loved being in his embrace. She felt safe. Nothing else in the world mattered. If she could she would've stayed in his arms forever. The sad part was that McKinley knew forever didn't exist for them. When they got to St. Louis she'd have to confess to Koran that the last few days they'd shared were all they had. It would hurt like hell, but it was something she had to do.

McKinley wasn't mentally, financially or spiritually ready to be with him yet. She had to get her life on track and come to grips with everything that had happened between her and Jamil before she could even think about being with another man. Her mind was too bogged down with all of the lies Jamil told and trying to decipher what was real between her and Jamil and what was fake.

She didn't have a job, let alone a dime to her name, and her soul was too wounded to trust any man. At that moment and stage in her life, McKinley had to give herself over to God first before she could think of jumping into another relationship. She just prayed that once she was in a place of stability, Koran would still be open and available to lend her his heart.

Finally, after days of mayhem and pure madness, McKinley and Koran made it to St. Louis. Both couldn't have been happier. They'd finally get to see their loved ones' faces. Outside, in front of the train station, McKinley nervously teetered from one foot to another. She could barely breathe. At any second Koran's cab or her mother would be arriving and she hadn't uttered a word to Koran about what she was feeling. Her mind knew that breaking things off with him before things got too deep was the best thing to do, but the notion made her feel like her chest was caving in.

"I know that look on your face," Koran interrupted her thoughts.

"Huh?" McKinley blinked.

"You haven't been yourself since we left Tennessee. What's on your mind?"

McKinley swallowed the huge lump in her throat and willed herself not to cry.

"What's wrong? Talk to me." Koran reached out for her hand.

"It's just that I really like you."

"I like you, too." He brushed her hair from out of her face. "So what's the problem?"

McKinley looked up to the sky as tears stung the brim of her eyes.

"The problem is that I wanna continue seeing you, but I can't be with anybody right now. I just got out of a three-year relationship that was built on a lie and insecurity and what do I have to show for it? Nothing. I put all of me in a man and in the end not only did he shit on me, but I lessened myself just to be with him. I put my whole entire life in that man's hands and look at me. I'm twenty-five years old and moving back in with my mama. I have to do things differently this time. And that means taking care of *me* before I can give myself to you."

"I ain't gon' front, I wish things could be different. My feelings are hurt, but I understand. But when you're ready, get at me." He reached for her phone and put his number in it.

McKinley knew that she should say something, but couldn't figure out the right words to express how she felt. It didn't help matters either that Koran's cab had arrived; therefore, officially putting an end to their cross-country affair.

"My cab is here. I guess I'll see you next lifetime."

"Bye." McKinley stepped forward and gave him a hug.

"Bye, McKinley." Koran hugged her back and kissed her on the cheek. "Don't make me wait too long." Koran reluctantly pulled away from her and picked up his bags.

McKinley stood back and watched with sadness in her eyes as Koran put his things in the trunk of the cab. Before hopping into the cab, Koran paused and looked at McKinley one last time. McKinley gazed back at him and forced a smile onto her face. Koran gave her a slight smile back and winked his eye. Seconds later, the cab pulled away from the curb and just like in the movies, McKinley stood on the sidewalk and watched until the cab disappeared into the sunset.

XoXo

"McKinley!" Kristen yelled from her car, waving her hand.

McKinley scanned the pick-up area at Miami International Airport until she spotted her friend. The two women locked eyes with one another and smiled. They hadn't seen each other in six months. McKinley happily walked across the parking lot with her suitcase in tow.

"Girl, look at you," Kristen exclaimed, getting out of the car. "You look so pretty."

McKinley's hair was filled with an abundance of spiral curls. She was dressed weather-appropriate in a grey sweatshirt, black mini-skirt and black combat boots.

"Thank you, so do you." McKinley hugged her friend tight.

"Girl, we got so much to catch up on," Kristen said, helping her place her bag in the trunk of the car.

"You know me and Tony broke up, right?"

"Yeah, you told me that about a month ago." McKinley got into the car.

"Well, now I'm seeing this guy named Rico and girl, he is so muthafuckin' sexy."

McKinley gazed out of the front windshield, trying her best to stay interested in Kristen's conversation, but where they were heading had her on edge. McKinley was going visit Jamil's grave. Yes, she'd gotten her life together by going to school for an associate's degree in fashion merchandising, holding down a job as a salesperson for a boutique, purchasing her first car and renting a cozy one-bedroom studio apartment, but she and Jamil still had unfinished business.

McKinley thought that by accomplishing her goals she would feel better and be able to move on with her life peacefully. But all of the anger and pain she had for Jamil still resided deep within her heart. After months of analyzing why she still felt that way she finally realized that she'd never gotten a chance to properly say good-bye.

She hadn't been able to attend the wake or the funeral because of the circumstances she'd been under. McKinley had been forced to move on without having any kind of closure. So here she was, back in Miami, praying to God that this experience would release all of the demons that haunted her day after day.

"We're here." Kristen pulled up to the curb.

McKinley looked around at the acres of grass and tombstones, remorsefully.

"His grave is right over there." Kristen pointed to her right.

She put the car in park. "You need me to go wit' you?"

"No. I need to do this on my own." McKinley inhaled deeply, then got out.

Each footstep she took felt as if she was walking on grass made of quicksand. For a second she wondered had she made the wrong decision. Maybe visiting Jamil would do her more harm then good. She was already having shortness of breath. Her palms were sweaty and her vision was blurred. But she had to get the feelings she harbored off of her chest.

McKinley stood in front of Jamil's grave. His name, birth date and death date caused her whole entire body to shake. McKinley could even feel her eyelashes shaking. Swallowing hard, she allowed the tears that had been stinging her eyes to fall gracefully down her rosy cheeks.

"I thought that when I got here I'd know exactly what I wanted to say to you. But being here with you only makes me feel more confused. You know, for the last six months I've been trying to figure out the point of our relationship. I've tried so hard to figure out why for three years you made me believe that you loved me and that we had a future.

I thought about it when I woke up, when I brushed my teeth, when I pee'd, when I sat in traffic, when I ate dinner alone. I thought about it so much that it made my head hurt. But you know what I realized?" She pulled out a tissue from her purse and wiped her nose.

"I realized that like everything else in your life I was just another game that you loved to play. You knew how I felt about you. You knew that I loved you and that I would do anything for you. You knew that I would never leave you and that's why you did every fucked-up thing under the sun to me." McKinley became angry.

"I let you get away with so much for so long that the shit you did became a big- ass joke to you. I should've known you weren't shit when you cheated on me twice, when you stood me up fifty-million times, when you gave me the silent treatment when you were the one who was wrong." She sniffled.

"I should've walked away from yo' ass then, but like a dummy I stayed 'cause I thought you would eventually change. I believed you every single time you sat in my face and told me that you wouldn't hurt me anymore. Every time you promised me you'd do better I prayed to God and I said, 'God, please let this time be different'." McKinley looked up at the sky and let her tears fall from out of the corners of her eyes.

"And every time," she looked back down at his headstone, "you made me out to look like a complete and utter idiot. You hurt me so much that it got to the point where I'd rather put up wit' your shit than be alone. My love for you became more important than my self-worth. I knew in my head that the way you treated me wasn't right, but I wanted to be with you and be in a relationship so bad that I made myself believe that the things you did to me were okay." She cried uncontrollably.

"I forgot that real love doesn't hurt all the time. Yeah, in a relationship you have problems, but we had a problem every other day. *Every* day." She stressed the word every. "When I woke up every morning, I'd wonder, *What's going to happen today?* With you I had to always be on guard 'cause I never knew what you were going to do next. Then, after I thought you'd done everything humanly possible to hurt me, you go and die on me. And I thought that was the worse, but then you sucker-punched me again." She threw up her hands then slapped them down onto her thighs.

"I learned that not only were you married with kids, but that you had a whole nother girlfriend and kids. Hell, I wasn't even your mistress. I was your number two girlfriend. So I guess you never had any intention on marrying me. You only proposed to me to keep me content a little while longer." She broke down and cried even harder.

After a short pause, McKinley wiped her eyes and inhaled deeply.

"I swear to God I wanna hate you so bad, but I can't." She shook her head.

"I'm just mad as hell at myself for letting things go on so long. But I'm here today, Jamil, to tell you that despite everything you've done to me. I still love you, but I'm letting you go." McKinley took her engagement ring out of her purse.

"There will be no more wondering and guessing what your intentions were 'cause it was what it was. You were a liar and you didn't mean me any good and that's all I need to know now." She placed the ring on top of his headstone, caught up in the moment.

Before walking away, McKinley took one last look at Jamil's grave. This would be the first and last time she'd ever visit him. It was now time for her to put the past behind her and move on to the good part of her life that God had in store for her. As she walked toward Kristen's car, McKinley quickly came to her senses and ran back over to Jamil's grave and picked up the ring.

"I may be dumb, but I ain't stupid. I can put this muthafucka on eBay."

Epilogue

After visiting Jamil's grave, life for McKinley got even easier. It was as if a weight had been lifted off of her shoulders. She was able to breathe again without feeling like she was going to be sick. Sleepless nights no longer existed. She was finally at a place of peace. But there was one thing she had left to do.

McKinley stood on the balcony of her apartment. The sun was out in full view. Birds were chirping and the leaves from the trees swayed in the wind. With her phone in her hand, McKinley said a silent prayer to God. *God, please don't let him have forgotten about me.* She dialed Koran's number. For the last six months she hadn't been able to get him out of her mind. She missed him dearly and couldn't wait to hear the sound of his voice again.

"Hello?" he answered in a low and raspy tone.

"Hi," McKinley uttered softly.

Koran held the phone close to his ear and smiled. He'd been waiting for this day for months.

"It took you long enough," he finally said.

"I know." McKinley laughed. "I miss you."

"I miss you, too."

"So when can I come see you?" Koran asked.

"The sooner, the better."

The Way It Is

**By Cat Eyez

Acknowledgements

I would be remiss in my duty to my Creator if I didn't thank Him first and foremost for blessing me to be in His great Universe alive and well. Thank You Heavenly Father.

I would like to acknowledge all those who have been by my side and who have supported me over the years. You know who you are. I want you to know you are appreciated.

I want to say to my "haters", or rather to those who just "misunderstand," a brother. You know, those who see me on a regular, her in the belly of the beast, who think I act funny because I don't want drink, or get high with you and don't want to indulge in foolishness that will keep a brother down in life and not up, I'm not in any way above anyone. I come from the bottom like all my brothers in the belly of the beast who are from the hood. Through the help of Almighty God in my life now, I see things differently. I see that I'm bigger than the devilish mentality I inherited from the streets. God doesn't give birth to "thugs". God gives birth to upright "thinkers"! It's only when we cut the bullsh**, and stop acting like men and start BEING men, that we will stay our ass out of prison and away from early graves! So if you want to say I act funny because I don't want to be ignorant anymore, cool. Roll with whatever blows your hair back. As for me though, I'm moving forward.

Shout out to my true Blackband Brothers because the community needs our leadership. Let's stand strong and help rebuild what we, through ignorance, help to destroy.

Lastly, I dedicate this book to a good brother of mine, "Calvin Morgan" (L.C.). Thank you for buying typewriter ribbon, so I could type my manuscript and thanks for encouraging me to continue to write; you are appreciated. Also, Marvin Graham, what up?

Finally to Keisha Ervin and Rose Jackson-Beavers, thank you for allowing me to take this journey with you. I appreciate you and wish nothing but happiness and success for you both.

THE WAY IT IS

1

YOU DON' BUMPED YOUR HEAD

"Ese muchacho va apprender que tene que respectar sus mallores." (That young man is gonna learn the hard way to respect his elders.) The Hispanic elderly man uttered to himself as he watched Derrick's car slowly passing by like it was a hearse in a funeral session. The young man was slumped down in the driver's seat and leaning sideways. He was sitting so low in his ride that only his dark-blue New York Yankee's baseball cap could be seen. His music was blasting hard and outrageously loud to rapper Jay Z's "Hard Knock Life," sending shockwaves through the neighborhood. It was Sunday morning and considered blatantly disrespectful by the elders and the religious communities for anyone to be blasting music as loud as Derrick's speakers were while church service was being conducted. Derrick, however, didn't give a damn. He looked over at the elderly Hispanic man and saw him fixing his face in an agitated fashion. The elderly man shook his head in the negative at Derrick's ill demeanor. Instead of Derrick refraining from interfering with the peace of the elderly man and church service that was being held at the church on the corner of the neighborhood, he gave the elderly man his middle finger and turned his music up even louder. "Boy, turn that music down. Haven't you any respect?" the elderly man yelled.

"Won't you put some teeth in your muthafuckin mouth?" Derrick shot back. *Fuckin' old folks always thinking a nigga gotta give them some respect. I ain't gotta do a damn thing. Fuck them!* he said to himself.

The elderly Hispanic man grabbed his cane, got up from his chair on his porch and went inside his house. "Yo tengo la edad para ser el padre del joven pero el me falta el respeto como si furea alguien de su edad. Perdonalo senor Dios."

(I am old enough to be the young man's father, but he disrespects me like I'm someone his age. Heavenly Father, forgive him.)

$$$$$

Derrick continued mobilizing through the hood. He was smoking on some of the greenest and potent weed on the west side of Charlotte, North Carolina, where there were more young black men roaming the hood without fathers in their lives than there were police patrolling the streets where the young men hustled. Derrick was one of them; a young man, eighteen years old to be exact, without a father figure in his life. He had just graduated the previous year from high school, and only had one thing on his mind—getting money. He certainly had reasons.

He took a left on Lanordo Street and parked in the lot of an apartment that rested right at the corner of Lanordo and Bivens Street. He killed his engine and exited his candy-apple-red chromed-out old-school Chevy Impala. He was wearing a white khaki polo shirt, blue jeans by Calvin Klein and all-white Air Force Ones. Derrick's jeans were so oversized that when he walked they fell below his buttocks. Had he been in a prison environment wearing his pants in such manner, some male looking for a young man to become his prison bitch would walk up to him without warning and touch him on his ass cheeks in hopes of having an intimate affair. Or, worse, rape him!

He took a deep drag from his marijuana cigarette, released the smoke from his nostrils after holding it in a few seconds, then said with both his hands lifted skyward: "The world is mines!" His little eleven-year-old brother, Mike-Mike, was sitting on the front steps of their apartment, playing with his basketball.

"Who are you now, Scarface?" his little brother said.

"Damn right. I'm Tony Muthafuckin' Montana!"

"Derrick, boy, you high. Betta not let Momma see—"

Before Mike-Mike could finish his sentence, their mother came out of their apartment. She marched toward Derrick, screaming, "I know you ain't smoking a blunt out here in my yard, Derrick." She reached for it. Although high as the sky, he managed to dodge her attempt. "You don' bumped your head for real. You know I don't pl—"

"I know, I know, Momma. You don't play that," he said, cutting her off and tossing the blunt somewhere into the lawn. "I really don't see what the fuss is all about though. It's just weed."

Arms folded, she repeated, "Just weed?"

"Yeah, Momma, just weed. A natural herb from the earth."

"I wouldn't give a fat baby's backside if it was only an Indian's peace pipe. You find somewhere else to puff on it! That stuff ain't doing nothing but killing your brain cells."

"A'ight then, whatever. If I wanted to hear a sermon I would have gon' to church," he muttered.

"What you say? I promise you, boy, I'll knock your teeth straight down your damn throat."

"Yeah, and I'll forget all about you, too," Derrick uttered to himself. "This woman needs a man in her life. Every day she finds something to trip about," he said, under his breath, walking toward Mike-Mike. He put his open palm on top of his little brother's forehead and slightly pushed it back. "What's up, knucklehead?"

"Nothing," replied Mike-Mike. "Just practicing my skills. I got a mean crossover, look."

Mike-Mike started dribbling his basketball around and in and out of his legs.

"Try to take the ball from me, Derrick."

Derrick positioned himself to take the ball, but when he reached for it; his little brother did a crossover move on him so smooth and sweet that Derrick nearly broke his ankle in his attempt to take the ball. "Okay, lil bruh. I see you got mad skills."

"Told you."

"Keep it up and you might end up in the NBA one day."

"Might?"

"You've gotta work hard also on your schoolwork. What your report card look like anyway?"

"I passed to the next grade. Didn't I, Momma?" Their mother was still standing there with her arms folded. Before she could reply, Mike-Mike added, "You know my birthday's tomorrow."

"And?"

"And you promised me that you were gonna buy me some Air Force Ones. The all-white ones like yours."

"Well, I lied. Now what?"

Mike-Mike sucked his teeth and made his sad face. "C'mon, now Derrick, you promised me that—"

"Have I ever made a promise to you that I didn't keep?" Derrick said, cutting him off.

"No, but you just said that you lied about getting me those Air Force Ones."

"Boy, you know I got you." Derrick then hit his little brother hard in his upper left arm.

"Ouchhh! Man, that hurt."

"Shut up and take it like a man. What I tell you about being all soft?"

Derrick's mother hit him hard in his chest. "And what I tell you about hitting him like that? He's a kid, not a punching bag."

"So what? That doesn't mean he gotta be soft. I don't want no soft, sugar-filled brother."

"Hitting him, Derrick, is not gonna make him hard or manly."

"With all due respect, Momma, how do you know? You're not a man."

"And you not his daddy. For your information, I don't have to be a man to know what one acts like. If you wanna do something, try being a positive example for him to follow. Now let me see you inside the house. I got a bone to pick with you."

Derrick immediately knew that something had to be wrong. Anytime his mother didn't want to talk to him about something in the presence of Mike-Mike, it was serious.

$$$$$

The Northside of Charlotte bred niggas who would bust a nigga's bubble for simply looking at a gangsta the wrong way. God forbid a nigga say the wrong thing out of his mouth. On that side of town, before the sun could grace the sky fully with its presence, a meeting was being conducted. Fat Jerome, a big-time drug dealer, had ordered two of his most ruthless hit men to meet him at a gambling house off 15th and Davison Ave. The two hit men were Tye-Tye and Rasco. Tye-Tye was known for cutting dudes throats and leaving 'em in the woods to bleed to death. And Rasco was known for putting his 9mm glock in his enemy's mouth and pulling the trigger. The two of them only did jobs for Fat Jerome.

They made Fat Jerome one of the most feared drug dealers to work for.

"Fellas, I requested this meeting because I got a lil problem on the Westside with an individual who I gave some coke to on consignment. I really didn't want to fuck with the kid, but Veronda convinced me."

"You talking 'bout lil fine-ass Veronda, the ex-stripper who used to run lil errands and shit for us, right?" asked Tye-Tye.

"Right. She fucks with the guy and asked me to front him something on her name. Since the bitch cool and shit, I hit the lil nigga off with a whole kilo."

"A kilo? Damn, Fat Jerome, you ain't never gave me a kilo of coke to hustle," interjected Rasco, scratching his arm like a junkie fiending for drugs.

His outburst made Fat Jerome mad. But because of a flight he had to catch, he kept his anger under control and said, "Cut the bullshit. You're a killa, not a damn drug dealer."

"Yeah, but…"

"Just play your position, dawg. You don't see the lungs in your body trying to do what your kidneys are responsible for doing, do you?"

"I'm just saying…"

"Nah, answer my question."

Rasco looked at Tye-Tye who kept his eyes on Fat Jerome. "You right, dawg," said Rasco. "You right."

"Precisely. Besides whether I give you coke to hustle or not, I still take care of you and Tye, don't I?"

"Fat Jerome, you take good care of us, trust me," interjected Tye-Tye. Tye-Tye didn't know why Rasco would fix his mouth to say what he said to Fat Jerome, because Fat Jerome had both of them eating good. In Tye-Tye's eyes there was no need to complain.

"Man, I was just throwing that out there, that's all," said Rasco. "No offense intended," he lied. Truth was, he not only wanted to do hits, he wanted to step his game up and become his own boss, so that he could do as he pleased, including drugs, if he wanted to.

"Do that shit on your own time. I got a fuckin' flight to catch," said Fat Jerome, trying to keep his anger on ice and chill. He hated being interrupted, especially for something frivolous, or for something that could have waited to be brought up some other time. He sighed, and then continued. "Now, that young cat I was telling y'all about, I was hitting him off good with coke, and the nigga never came up short with my cheese 'til here recently. I shot him a block last month and haven't heard from him since."

"The nigga hasn't called you or nothing?" asked Tye-

Tye.

"He hasn't done shit. In fact, I tried his and Veronda's cell phone number. Both of their numbers changed. And Veronda ain't living at the same address she was living at prior to this shit."

"So I guess this young nigga call himself not paying you then, huh?" said Tye.

"Precisely. Which means we gotta straight punish his ass. If the nigga feels like his balls are that big to fuck me, then it's time to show him how we crack balls that big."

Rasco cracked his knuckles and said, "Oh fo'sho, my nigga."

Fat Jerome threw him the keys to his Hummer, and tossed him a see-through small ziplock bag full of chronic. "Put that underneath my driver's side seat." While Rasco went to do so, Fat Jerome motioned with his head for Tye-Tye to lag behind. When Rasco was clearly out of sight, Fat Jerome said to Tye-Tye, "Rasco's loyalty is questionable, and we can't have that. Plus, I heard from a reliable source that the nigga don' started smoking crack. This, you and I both know, is a violation in our crew." One of Fat Jerome's rules for those of his Cash Money Click was "No getting high." No getting high off their supply or anyone else's. Fat Jerome believed that drugs like coke and heroin clouded a street soldier's vision. So, drug use was strictly prohibited.

"Nah, we don't do that shit. That's for the junkies. But is this shit true, though?" Tye-Tye shot back.

"It's true. And remember when my dope house in Matthews North Carolina got robbed?"

"Yeah, I remember you telling me about that shit," Tye-Tye responded, with his nose spread and a mean street grit on his face.

"Word is, his ass is the one who set that shit up. The nigga who told me said that Rasco came to him first and asked him if he wanted to make some fast cash. He told the dude what was up, but when the dude found out that Rasco wanted him to rob a spot that belonged to me, he refused. This same nigga smoke weed laced with crack. He said he and Rasco don' smoked that shit numerous times together."

"So why is this coming to the surface now, Fat Jerome? Matter of fact, where is this nigga who told you all this?"

"I heard the nigga got popped coming back from Miami somewhere. His name was Short-Arm."

"I know that nigga. He has been missing about a good-ass seven or eight months."

"Precisely. The reason I didn't say anything is because I wanted to give Rasco the benefit of the doubt. But when the nigga screamed just a moment ago about me not ever giving him any crack to sell, he made me fuckin' angry. He's a nigga we no longer need, therefore, see his ass, because, Tye, little violations left uncheck leads to big ones. Rasco is a snake. And some snakes don't rattle. That's what makes them so deadly."

"I'll holler at him ASAP," replied Tye-Tye.

"Precisely. And do it the thug way," said Fat Jerome as the two of them parted company.

Fat Jerome was a thirty-five-year-old drug dealer who believed in unity. He hated dishonest, disloyal street soldiers. He knew that a house divided couldn't stand. Therefore, weak links had to be eliminated regardless of the major love one might have for that weak link. He loved Rasco, because it was Rasco who saved his ass from catching a sexually transmitted disease. At the time, he didn't know Rasco, nor did Rasco know him. Rasco had only heard of Fat Jerome as a dude whose name was ringing all over the Queen City for being deep in the game. While at a strip club one night, though, Rasco saw this real big, fat-ass dude—six-foot-three and every bit of 300 pounds—standing in front of the stage that the strippers were doing their dances on. The fat dude was light-skinned with long dread locks that hung far down the middle of his back. On his wrist was a diamond bezel platinum Rolex watch that sparkled every time lights from the club reflected off of it. In the fat man's hands were stacks of cash that he handed out to the strippers who twirled booty and pussy in his face. One of the girls, who stripped and danced before the fat man, was a chick Rasco knew well. Her name was Jessica. A white chick with a fat ass who had death on her pussy. Rasco knew her from high school. She had syphilis, the same STD that put Gangster and Mob Boss Alcapone's dick in the dirt. Before Jessica could drop to her knees to give the fat man some head, Rasco interrupted, "Yo, Big Man, trust me, you don't want this bitch sucking your dick. The bitch got syphilis."

The fat man looked at Rasco, "Yo, who the fuck are you and how did you get in here?" he questioned, realizing Rasco had entered the VIP room invited.

"I know the club owner, dawg. Regardless of that, this here bitch got death on her pussy. Ain't that fuckin' right, Jessica?"

"Nigga, you lying like the devil," she shot back, getting up from her knees.

"I'm lying?" Rasco repeated. He then grabbed her by the back of her hair. "Bitch, if I'm lying then this lying-ass nigga 'bout to blow your brains out 'cause you know your pussy got death on it." He slipped his 9mm out from his waist and positioned it at her head.

"Hold. Hold on, yo. Put your gun away, bro, and let the ho go," the fat man ordered.

Rasco pushed her head hard toward the door, and kicked her in her ass. "Stankin' ass bitch! You know that pussy between your legs would send a nigga to his grave. I hate y'all kind of bitches."

"You just a hater," she shouted, before storming out of VIP and slamming the door behind her.

Rasco put his gun away, looked at the fat man, and said, "Excuse me, Big Man, for the interruption, but that bitch dirty. You look like a cool dude, so I just wanted to warn you."

"Dayum, man, for a minute I didn't know what the fuck was going on. I appreciate you, though, shit. By the way, I'm Fat Jerome."

"Nice to meet you, Fat Jerome. If you ever need a true soldier in your corner, I'm available," Rasco assured. Fat Jerome had a lot of soldiers that rolled with him. He honestly didn't need any more. However, it was something about this five-foot-eleven, dark-skinned slim soldier, Rasco, that Fat Jerome liked. It was the fact that Rasco had just aggressively saved his life and was extremely bold about it. That was enough to make Rasco a part of his money-making team. Since Rasco was aggressive and wasn't afraid to use a gun, Fat Jerome linked him up with Tye-Tye and the both of them were used as hit men.

All Fat Jerome wanted any soldier in his crew to do was simply play their position and the family would continue to get money. He didn't want killers in his crew selling drugs, because all his killers had quick tempers. No one with a quick temper and short fuse would make a good drug dealer, because the very moment someone came up short with cash, those quick-tempered killers would have bodies all over Queen City.

Being a drug dealer meant compromising sometimes. So, Fat Jerome did his best to keep his soldiers in their rightful place. Rasco wanted to evolve though. When he secretly robbed one of his boss man's drug houses, as well as started secretly smoking crack, and now a sudden outburst at an important meeting, he had proven himself to be a problem. A problem that Tye-Tye was now ordered to solve.

$$$$$

Derrick followed his mother into her bedroom and closed the door behind him. His mother went straight to her closest and retrieved a large-sized brown paperbag. She tossed it onto her bed. Derrick immediately knew what it contained.

"What in the hell have I told you about bringing this garbage where we lay our heads, huh, Derrick? This stuff was sitting right out on my living-room sofa where Mike-Mike could have very well gotten to it."

"Momma, I'm sorry. I forg—"

"I don't want to hear you forgot. You know, if those Housing Authority folks were to come and do an unexpected inspection of our apartment and find that garbage in here, what's gonna happen?"

Derrick inhaled and exhaled hard. "I promise you, Momma, it won't happen again."

"Don't make promises you don't intend to keep. You can't even manage to keep your mind clear enough to think right. Look at you, you stay high on that weed stuff, twenty-four/seven; you swore up and down when you graduated a year ago that you were either going to the military, or you would enroll in barber college. You have done neither. Instead, you come in every night with large amounts of money you made off of selling that crack cocaine garbage. You try spoiling Mike-Mike with that drug money by buying him things. But I work hard every day to ensure that we have something—"

"Something like what, Momma? A government apartment to stay in?" Derrick said, cutting her off. "I'm sick and tired of the hood. All I've ever known is the hood. That's all my little brother knows as well. If we continue staying here, both me and my brother will do nothing but eventually become products of our environment. Yes, I was gonna go in the military, but since President Bush took office, the majority of the young males entering the military get deployed to Iraq, and are coming home in body bags. So I had to rethink going into the military. Barber school, well, I still might pursue that."

"I can't tell."

"You can't tell, Momma, because you're too busy pointing out the wrong that I do, without first seeing what it is I'm trying to accomplish."

Derrick was sick and tired of what living in the hood reminded him of, as well as how it made him feel on a constant basis. Living in the hood reminded him daily that he, his mother, and his little brother, Mike-Mike were poor. As a result of their poverty, they had to be assisted by a government in which Derrick believed had never had poor people's best interest at heart. Especially poor black people. As far as Derrick was concerned, the government, through its welfare program, caused many single mothers to sit around idle and wait for a support check every month. And even though Derrick's mother worked, she had to do so undercover, without the government knowing about it, because if she made more money on her job than the government allowed, the government would terminate her welfare benefits in a hurry. In addition, Derrick hated the fact that while his father was alive, his father was not allowed by the government to stay with them at their apartment, as long as his mother was being assisted by welfare. That, Derrick believed, affected their family's stability. He felt that instead of the government disallowing his father to stay with them, the government should have promoted it for the purpose of their family staying together.

His father was sick with a chronic drug addiction. Heroin was his father's drug of choice, only because his father was unable to cope with some tragedies he witnessed while serving in the United States Marines. His father suffered from Post-Traumatic Stress Disorder. After his failed attempt at receiving veteran benefits, his heroin use increased. Living in the hood reminded young Derrick of all of this, and more. All he wanted was just to get the hell up out of such. If not for his sake, for his little brother and their mother's. If only he could get his mother to understand this.

"Listen here, young man, I don't care what you are trying to accomplish," Derrick's mother, getting directly up in his face. "You are my child, and I refuse to see you on the damn six o'clock news somewhere. Look at what happened to your father."

"Momma, you don't have to keep reminding me about what happened to my daddy. I know he was found in an alley with a needle in his arm. Besides, I'm not on drugs."

"You think you have to be on drugs to be a victim of what drugs can do, Derrick? If so, then who's being naive?"

Derrick sucked his teeth, placed his brown paper bag full of ready-to-sell cocaine underneath his armpit and was about to leave.

"Don't you walk away from me when I'm talking to you, Derrick," his mother shouted. Derrick had tears in his eyes. He hated to be reminded of his father's absence. Even though he was only an eight-year-old kid when his father died, he still remembered his father sitting him on his lap, telling him that he loved him and kissing him on his forehead, which always made him feel good.

"Momma, I'm just doing what I gotta do to help us get out the hood. Why can't you just accept that?"

"'Cause you still a kid, that's why."

"Momma, I'm almost nineteen."

"I wouldn't care if you were almost a hundred. You'll never be older than me. Now, I apologize for reminding you of your father. But listen here, those streets and those drugs will take you under. I see it all the time. Every day on the news some mother is crying because her child has gotten shot down either from gang violence, or from just being a part of the drug game. Do you know what it means to a mother to lose a child? I think not because you're not one."

"But Momma—"

"No, don't 'but Momma' me! That drug game, boy, is nothing but one gigantic mirage that's full of illusions. It all leads down the same path, a one-way street to destruction with no fork in the road."

Derrick sighed. *Here she go with the preachin' again*, he thought to himself.

"You right, Momma."

"No, I don't need you to affirm whether I'm right or wrong. I need for you to clean your act up, and not bring that garbage back into our house."

"You mean this government apartment?"

"Whatever. You ought to be thankful you got a roof over your head. Some people ain't got that. If you had it your way; you, me and Mike-Mike would be sleeping out in the streets."

"We would be sleepin' out in the streets? Why would you say that when I'm doing everything in my power to help get us into our own home, Momma?"

"You doing everything, but the right thing. 'Cause like I said, if those Housing Authority folks were to do an unexpected inspection here, ain't no tellin' what they would find *illegal* of yours. Those drugs in that paper bag underneath your arm, anybody could have spotted it in our living room. But you stay so high off of that weed you constantly smoke, that you don't even know where you be placing that stuff. All I'm telling you is, don't bring that stuff back in here. Derrick, I mean that! Now get it out of here!"

Derrick's mother was a strict no-nonsense woman. She wanted the best for both of her sons. But raising two boys wasn't easy at all. She was a forty-seven-year-old, high-school dropout whose only income was a once-a-month government check and the pay she received weekly from working for an elderly retired doctor as a housekeeper. Every dime she earned went toward purchasing food, clothing, paying her car off and other little things necessary for her, Mike-Mike and Derrick. Derrick often refused to let her buy him anything. After he started hustling coke, he insisted on purchasing things for her and Mike-Mike. The few times Derrick tried giving his mother large amounts of cash, she refused to accept it. She told him she didn't accept dirty money.

"There is no such thing as dirty money," Derrick always responded. But in his mother's eyes, money earned the illegal way was money she didn't want to spend, let alone have in her possession. "Well, Momma, the money you make without the government knowing about it, what kind of money is that? Is it legal, or illegal?" Derrick once asked his mother.

"It's money I earn the honest way. I just don't report it because the government will raise my rent." Derrick knew the government would indeed raise his mother's rent if she reported that she was working and the job was paying her pretty nicely.

Still Derrick laughed hard at her reply and said, "Momma, you got game."

"Whateva."

2

I DON'T GIVE A FUCK ABOUT FAT JEROME

Derrick left his mother's apartment, jumped into his ride and hit the highway.

He did so with the express intent of never bringing cocaine into his mother's place again. He knew she would verbally spank his ass for his carelessness of leaving his money-making product out as he did. For that, he felt somewhat ashamed. He pulled up at his girlfriend Veronda's crib. He exited his car with his brown paper bag underneath his armpit. He hit the doorbell and after waiting a minute or two, Veronda answered.

"Hey, baby. I didn't know you were coming over," she said, standing before him in her white T and tight booty shorts.

"Neither did I, this early," he responded, sidestepping her to enter into her living room. Usually he would greet her with a kiss, but his mother checking him for slipping had him a little discombobulated.

"My mom's fuckin' trippin'," he continued.

"'Bout what?"

"'Bout this." Derrick tossed her the brown paperbag.

eronda caught it and took a peek inside. "Hell, no wonder, boo. You know damn well your mom don't play with you selling drugs."

"I fucked up and left the shit laying out on the sofa in her living room."

"That's even worse. I know that lil pretty mother of yours pitched a fit."

"She did everything, but shoot my ass."

"Shit, if she had a gun I'm sure she would've," replied Veronda, laughing.

"Threatened to knock my teeth down my throat and everything."

"You gon' run your mother crazy, Derrick, I swear."

"Not on purpose, Veronda. Look, all I'm trying to do is fuckin' get us out the damn hood."

"You will eventually, baby. Rome wasn't built in a night. Neither were the Egyptian pyramids."

"I know that."

"Slow down then," she said, caressing his face with her hand.

"I can't fuckin' move at a snail's pace on this one. It's now or never. 'Cause the hood I stay in ain't got nothing but a bunch of fuckin' drug dealers, robbers and pimps in there. Everyday my little brother walks home from school and he has to witness this shit. I know, because I had to witness it, too, when I was his age. Now, look at what I've become, a damn drug dealer. Someone I said I would never become. Now ain't that a bitch?"

"Life's a bitch, depending on how you dress her. Like I said, baby boy, in time you will have what it is you seek. That is, if you don't get careless and start moving too fast."

"I'm just tired of this hood bullshit."

"I can dig it, Derrick. Besides where the hell you think I'm from? I'm just saying take it slow."

"Speaking of the hood, though. You ever wonder why they never call the projects a neighborhood? You know, like rich people stay in a neighborhood. But the poor, the hood."

"I've never really given it any thought," replied Veronda. "Why you think it's like that?"

"I think it's like that, because poor people, particularly black poor people, we always getting the 'ass end' of every damn thing! They remove neighbor and give us hood. A fuckin' hood is defined as something that goes over one's head. This shit is a trip."

"Boy, you too much. You always thinking and coming up with something."

"Naw, I'm just keeping it real, Veronda. I'm just keepin' it fuckin' real."

"You definitely got a point, though. But peep this. You know you also got your hands full with this Fat Jerome thang, right?"

"Veronda, for real-for real, I don't give a fuck about Fat Jerome, or the lil niggas that work for that muthafuckah!"

"I know but—"

"But what? Shit, ain't nothing to discuss about that fat muthafuckah. After what you told me he did to you, I had a right to take his coke. The pig's lucky I didn't take his life."

"Boo, don't talk like that."

"What, you getting soft on me, Veronda?"

"No."

"That fat nigga took you over to his place, got you pissy drunk and when you awoke you discovered that the fat bitch had sodomized you. I understand you didn't want to break the G-code of the streets, but for real-for real you should have went and took out a warrant on his ass."

"He would have only gotten out, then my life really would have been in danger. See, Derrick, I've been knowing Fat for a while. I know what he is capable of doing. Well, not him, but the lil goons that run with him. Especially Rasco and Tye-Tye. They'll do anything for him, no bullshit."

"Them niggas aren't the only ones that'll hurt something," Derrick shot back.

"That's not what I'm indicating. All I'm saying is Fat Jerome is not gonna sit around idly, knowing someone has failed to pay him, and do nothing."

"Look, the fact remains, the nigga was wrong for what he did to you. Doing that to you was like him doing it to me. Shit, he knew you were my girl when he did it. That's like me laughing and grinning in his face daily, then, when he turn his back, I snatch the chick he care about and screw her. Now, how would that look, and he and I supposed to be business associates? I never once failed to pay him. I only decided not to give him shit after what you told me you suspected he did to you."

"Not suspected. The nigga did it to me," Veronda corrected.

"Well, he fucked you, and I fucked him. Whatever he wants to do about it, we can do it. 'Cause, honestly, I don't give a fuck. Besides, is my Forty-Four Desert Eagle still in your closet?"

"You know I'm afraid of guns, Derrick. So, if you placed it in my closet it's definitely still there."

"Good."

Derrick walked into Veronda's bedroom. He went straight to her closet while she placed the paper bag full of coke underneath her mattress. When Veronda looked up, she saw Derrick placing bullets in the clip of his gun. "What you plan on doing with that, Derrick? I hope nothing stupid."

"I ain't gonna do anything stupid. I'm just strapping up because you're right; that fat muthafuckah just might come looking for me. If in the event that he does, all I can say is, the big nigga betta come correct."

"Or?" replied Veronda.

"Or somebody will pay a severe fuckin' price."

Derrick wasn't a hard-as-hell street gangstah who strived on looking for trouble. He was in the streets to stack paper, not to start problems. Derrick wasn't a punk either. He knew beyond a doubt that being soft in the game meant getting pushed around, or pushed over. Neither would happen if Derrick could help it. So, when he started selling drugs, one of the first things he did was purchase him a gun. Guns were easy to come across in the hood, and damn near every hustler and bad boy had one. With Fat Jerome and his goons looking for him, Derrick figured it was time he'd carry his gun on him everywhere he went. He couldn't chance slipping, because slipping on Fat Jerome and his crew could equate to a death sentence, and Derrick wasn't ready to die.

$$$$$

It was 11:45 P.M., and Fat Jerome's two hit men, Tye-Tye and Rasco, mobilized through the Westside searching with eagle eyes for their eighteen-year-old target.

"We've been riding and looking for this young nigga damn

near all night, Tye-Tye. And everybody we've asked over here on the Westside act like they don't know who this nigga is, man," said Rasco.

"Somebody knows who he is, we just gotta be patient. You know how them young cats are. They get out here in these streets and start hustling and making a lil money and the first thing they want is a lil attention on their asses," replied Tye-Tye, who had more than killing Derrick on his mind.

"Tell me 'bout it," Rasco said.

"So they go buy the biggest and the nicest car their drug money can buy. They gotta have all the jewelry and half of them carry money around in their pockets, like their pocket is a bank, or something. These niggas stupid. Stupidity causes a nigga to slip sooner or later."

"You right about that, Tye. Stupidity is a muthafuckah. You sho' right."

"I know I am. Not just that, though. The majority of the young cats you see hustling out here, when the cops roll down on them the first thing they do is start rattin' on their friends and shit."

"Yep," replied Rasco.

"I know ain't none of us out here perfect and shit, but if you gon' be a gangsta, be a gangsta. Rattin' to the cops about what goes on in the streets ain't cool at all."

"Naw, that rattin' shit ain't cool, dawg. That shit ain't cool at all."

"Neither is getting out of line with someone who puts money in your pocket and food on your table," Tye-Tye said.

When Tye-Tye said that, Rasco embraced silence a moment, then he said, "What you mean by that, Tye-Tye?"

Tye-Tye was too mad to explain himself. "Hold on a minute, I gotta take a leak." Tye-Tye pulled his car over to the side of a lonely dirt road, surrounded by trees. "I'll be back." Tye-Tye got out the car, took a leak and headed back to the car. Instead of heading back to the driver's side, he walked straight up to the passenger side. He opened the door in a hurry, yanked Rasco out and cut Rasco's throat from one end of his neck to the other. It happened so fast that Rasco didn't stand a fighting chance.

"You're a snake-ass nigga." Tye-Tye watched Rasco struggle for air. "Don't fight it, muthafuckah, it's over, all fuckin' over. You talk too damn much."

To bite the hand that feed you in the streets was a violation of the gangstah code of loyalty. For a nigga to have an unbridled tongue was damn near equally the same, especially when the unbridled tongue talked bullshit in the midst of the bossman conducting business.

Tye-Tye followed up on what his boss ordered him to do. He took Rasco's life like it was no problem, wiped his blood-stained weapon over Rasco's clothing and left him on the side of a lonely dirt road. He then got back into his car as if nothing had happened and continued his search for Derrick.

$$$$$

3

HAPPY BIRTHDAY, LIL MIKE

MONDAY AFTERNOON

"Where you get all of that money from, bruh, if you don't work?" asked Mike-Mike, as he stepped into Derrick's bedroom. He didn't hear Mike-Mike approach because his music was up loud.

"Don't worry about all that. What I tell you about being so nosy, anyway?"

"I wasn't being nosy. You had your door cracked—"

"Regardless. What you doing looking in here. Do you sleep in here?"

"No, but—"

"But nothing." His little brother was about to walk away. "Come here, and shut my door behind you." Mike-Mike did as Derrick ordered. "How did you like your lil birthday present I bought you?" he asked. He turned the volume down on NWA's *Fuck the Police* CD.

"Which one?"

"The one around your neck." Derrick bought Mike-Mike a diamond-cut rope chain with a Nike medallion. Mike-Mike reached for it and held it by the medallion. "I love this chain, bruh; it's nice."

"You betta, I paid twelve hundred dollars for it."

"Twelve hundred dollars? That's more than the Air Force Ones

22222

you bought me."

"I know. Don't tell Momma, though, a'ight?"

"I won't."

"Why were you and Momma arguing yesterday?"

"That's between Momma and me. Everything's fine though."

"When you left, I saw Momma in her room on her knees, praying and crying. I even heard her say in her prayer, God, I'm putting my son in your hands. Who was she talking about, bruh? Me or you?"

"Probably you, Mike-Mike."

"Me? What I do?"

"Nah, Momma mad at me right now. You really wanna know why?"

"Why?"

"Well, lil bruh, since you twelve years old today, I can start sharing more things with you. Momma mad at me because I do illegal things to make my money."

"Like what?"

Like things I shouldn't be doing, and betta never ever see you doing."

"Like selling drugs?"

"Something like that. But anyway, she hates that I do illegal things."

"Why you do those things, bruh, if you know that the things you're doing will hurt her?"

Derrick put away his cash. "I don't mean to hurt Momma. I love Momma. But I love also doing what I gotta do to try to help us get out the hood. Little bruh, I hate the hood. Ain't nothing in the hood but poverty and more poverty. If it kills me, I gotta do what I gotta do to help get us out of here."

"Momma said that by this time next year we gonna be moving into a house of our own?"

"I can't wait 'til next year. I wanna see us in our own house in a matter of months. And that's exactly what's gonna happen if things line up with how I have planned them. Now, besides all that, your Air Force Ones look good on your feet. Thought I wasn't gonna get them for you, didn't you?"

"Not really. I know you always look out for me, 'preciate it, too."

Derrick placed his hand on top of Mike-Mike's head and said, "No problem. I want you to have everything that I was deprived of when I was your age. And make no mistake about it, little bruh, I'll do whatever I have to do to see you with what you like."

Mike-Mike put his arms around Derrick's waist. He really loved his big brother.

"Guess what Momma bought me for my birthday? Well, you probably already know."

"No I don't. What she get you?"

"Guess."

"A new basketball?"

"Nope."

"A new video game?"

"Nope, got enough of those."

What she getcha then?"

"A brand new computer."

"Yeahhh?"

"Yep, a laptop. She said that she wanted me to be more than a basketball player. She says she wants me to be a lawyer."

"What do *you* wanna be? 'Cause at the end of the day, it's gonna be up to you."

"I don't know. But I think I want to be more like you, someone who will do any and everything to see his family in a better situation."

"I think you can do that being a lawyer, Mike-Mike. Now let's take a ride. I got one other present for you for your birthday."

"Another present?"

"Definitely. You gon' really enjoy this one."

"Oh, yeah, Momma told me to tell you to call her at work when you came in. She had to get to work early. That's why she wasn't here when you arrived."

"Okay, I'll call her from my cell phone. Let's go."

$$\$\$\$\$\$$

Derrick's car pulled up at Veronda's apartment. When Veronda came out, the first thing lil Mike-Mike said was, "Ain't that your girlfriend, bruh?"

"You betta believe it," replied Derrick.

"Man, she's fine. I remember when you brought her to our house. She's fine."

"You think so?"

"Know so."

Veronda stepped to the driver's side of the car, wearing an all-black, skintight, full body skirt, with some all-black stiletto heels. She had the legs and calves of an Olympic marathon runner. Her hair was long and curly like she was mixed with Indian and black. Her skin was caramel and her eyes were a pretty hazel—any man would melt looking into them. Lil Mike-Mike was instantly in love, just like Derrick was when he first saw her shaking her booty at a strip club.

"Hey, baby," she said, kissing Derrick on his lips. "What you up to?"

"Just hanging out with my lil brother, Mike-Mike. Today is his birthday."

"Really?" replied Veronda, looking over at Mike-Mike.

"Yep."

"Happy Birthday lil Mike," she said.

"Thank you." Mike-Mike replied, smiling.

"Baby, don't you got something for my lil brother?" Derrick said, smiling and winking his eye.

"Sure do," she replied, then walked around to where Mike-Mike was. She kissed him right smack dead on his lips. Mike-Mike's heart skipped a beat. He looked over at Derrick and smiled.

"Don't look at me," said Derrick. "She's the one who kissed you, not me. What you say to a kiss like that?"

Mike-Mike shrugged his shoulders and said, "I don't know."

"You say, can I please get another one?"

Mike-Mike looked at Veronda with a smile. "Can I please get another one?"

Veronda poked her lips out for him to kiss her.

"Mmmmm-mah," she uttered, as their lips touched again.

"Now c'mon let's go inside," said Derrick. The three of them headed inside. Once inside, Veronda told Mike-Mike to have a seat. Mike-Mike took a seat on the sofa. As he did so, he witnessed Derrick whispering something in Veronda's ear. He didn't know what Derrick was saying to her. But Mike-Mike noticed she was smiling at him the whole time Derrick was whispering in her ear.

"Have you ever had sex, Mike-Mike?" Veronda asked, as she came and sat next to him on the sofa.

Mike-Mike shook his head. "Nope, I've never had sex. My mother told me that I should wait until I get married."

Veronda looked back at Derrick.

"That's only if it's not your birthday. Besides, Momma ain't here," said Derrick, rolling up a blunt. "Now take your pants down, Veronda has a surprise for you."

Mike-Mike did as his brother said. He pulled both his pants and underwear down and sat back down on the sofa.

"Relax, okay Mike-Mike?" assured Veronda.

Mike-Mike laid back on the couch. Veronda bent over with one knee on the couch, massaged his dick 'til it was solid hard, then placed her mouth over it and licked around the head of it like it was her favorite-flavored lollipop. Mike-Mike closed his eyes and inhaled air through his teeth. Derrick puffed on his blunt and watched the birthday boy enjoy himself. "How does it feel, lil bruh? Do you like it?" he asked, releasing weed smoke from his lung.

"It feels goooood. Ooooo…"

Veronda stopped only to stop herself from laughing hard. She then said, "Hush, Derrick and let little brother allow me to light the fire on his candle."

"You got that, boo-boo." Veronda again placed her whole mouth on and over Mike-Mike's hard dick. She tightened her jaws and started moving her tongue around and around on his dick.

"Der-rick, B-b-bruh, this isss a-a-ama-zing."

Derrick took a hard drag from his blunt, then put it in an ashtray. "I know it feels amazing; I'm really getting jealous," he said as he eased up behind Veronda. He placed his hand underneath her skirt, slid her panties to the side and started rubbing up, down and around her clit and fingering her spot. Derrick's could tell by the way Veronda was moaning as his finger moved inside her tight wet hole. She seemed to have a difficult time giving Mike-Mike head. "Stay focused, baby. Stay focused," Derrick commanded. Mike-Mike had a confused look on his face like he didn't know whether to pay attention to what his brother was doing behind Veronda, or pay attention to Veronda's mouth moving up and down on his dick, making him feel good. So he made up his mind and did neither.

Instead, he laid his head back, closed his eyes and enjoyed the ride. Veronda looked up at Mike-Mike as she pulled her skirt up to her back. Derrick knew emphatically that this was an indication for him to slide every bit of his eight-and-a-half-inch, thick, hard dick inside her. He did so without delay, holding her panties to the side in the process. He started deep dickin' her slowly.

"Mmmmm," she moaned. Derrick stroked her pussy so good she nearly bit down on Mike-Mike's.

How in the hell could Fat Jerome have wanted to fuck my bitch up her asshole when her pussy hole is so muthafuckin on fire? This bitch of mines got the best snapper in Charlotte.

"Der-rrrrick, bruh, what is this I'm feeeeeling? It tickles."

"You're feeling what I'm feeling, lil bruh. It's called 'nuttin.' It's one of the greatest feelings you'll ever feel in your life. Enjoy it; it'll only last a few seconds."

"Derrick, you crazy, boy." Veronda laughed. "Now I gotta take another bath."

"Clean my little brother up, too, boo-boo."

"I got him," she replied, "Hold on. Stay there a minute, Mike-Mike, I'll be right back." Veronda returned with some baby wipes. She cleaned Mike-Mike up, kissed him on the cheek and said, "Once again, Happy Birthday!"

Mike-Mike just stood there. He was dazed from the head she had just given him. Never had he experienced an orgasm. Veronda had delivered him his first.

"What you say to that, Mike-Mike?" asked Derrick.

"I-I-I don't know."

"You say, Miss Veronda, that felt good. Can you do it to me again before I leave to go home?"

"Miss Veronda, that felt good. Can you—?"

Veronda cut him off with a laugh and said, "Maybe next year on your birthday."

"Tell her thank you, anyway," said Derrick.

"Thank you, Ver-Ve-ronda."

Veronda blew him a kiss. "You're welcome, handsome."

Derrick then looked at Mike-Mike and said, "Wait on me in the car. I'll be there in a second."

Mike-Mike exited. When he did, Derrick told Veronda to get his coke out the stash. As she followed up on his request, he went into the bathroom to wash his dick.

There was no way he was gonna be mobilizing around in the Queen City, smelling like pussy.

He walked into Veronda's bedroom. "Here you go," stated Veronda, handing him his bag full of coke.

As she stood before him, he cupped her ass cheek, kissed her on her top lip then her bottom and said, "Thank you for fuckin' rockin' my lil brother's world. Shit, I know he'll never forget you or that good-ass head you delivered."

Veronda smiled shyly, "You crazy, Derrick boy, I'm serious. You cra-zy."

"Here, take this and go to the mall," he said, pulling a wad of cash from one of his front pockets. He peeled off twelve hundred dollars.

"Thank you, boo-boo. Now, when am I gonna see you again?" Veronda asked.

"Later."

"What's later, Derrick?"

"I can't give you a definite, baby. I'll just pop up when I pop up."

"Why can't you just give me a definite? You always say that shit."

"'Cause the streets don't allow you to give definites. I'm caught up in this world of sin, motivated by dividends. Anything could fuckin' happen and you know that. But if in the process of me doing wrong out here in these streets, I happen to make it another minute, hour or day, I count it a blessing from the Big Man upstairs. You do know He looks out for thugs, too, right?"

"Derrick, God looks out for us all. For how long is the question."

"Well, hopefully, forever. Now, I'll be back later, baby. Don't worry," Derrick said between kisses and squeezing her booty. Veronda's booty felt like cotton in his hands, it was so soft. Had it not been for him having to get Mike-Mike back home, and him needing to get rid of the coke, he would have put that dick back up in her again. Instead, he tucked his bag of coke in his pants, checked for his gun at his waist, and bounced.

4

DON'T TELL MOMMA

"Derrick, bruh, this has been the best birthday of my life. Man, I'm for real," exclaimed Mike-Mike. He was so excited about getting his dick sucked.

Derrick smiled. "You really enjoyed yourself, huh?"

"Did I? Man, bruh, your girlfriend is amazing. I see why you in love with her."

"Well, I'm glad you're happy about that. It makes me feel good when I see you happy. When I was your age, very few things made me happy. But I didn't go around trippin' and whatnot about it. I did what Momma wanted me to do, which was concentrate hard on my school work. I'm out of school now. I walked across that stage with honor. Seeing the smile on Momma's face when I did so, was more fulfilling to me than actually receiving my diploma. She always stayed on me about finishing school, like I stay on you, Mike-Mike. She wanted me to do other things like join the military, but sometimes things don't always go as we want them to. You feel me, Mike-Mike?"

"I think so."

"But you…you gotta finish school. A young black man ain't got no place in this society without a good education. Even if you've got a good education, the cards are still somewhat stacked against you because of your skin color."

"My skin color? What you mean by that, bruh?"

"What I mean is, there are some people who think they are

better than you because they're white. See Mike-Mike, many years ago, our forefathers were kidnapped, by white thugs, and brought over here to America from our homeland, Africa. Our forefathers were brought here to be made slaves. Under the white thug slave owners' system, our forefathers were stripped of a lot of things."

"Stripped of a lot of things like what, bruh?"

"They were stripped of things like the knowledge of God, their identity, their culture and just their basic way of life."

"Why would a people do this to another people? Isn't such treatment of human beings considered a crime?"

"That type of treatment of people today is a crime, because slavery has been abolished. You do know who abolished slavery, don't you?"

"Of course. Abraham Lincoln, in what, eighteen-sixty-three, with the signing of the Emancipation Proclamation?"

"Right. But the slaves weren't set free until eighteen-sixty-five. To answer your question as to 'why would a people do this to another people?' Well, lil bruh, I don't have all the answers, but I can say this, some people are just straight-up evil. They judge you by the color of your skin, rather than judge you by the content of your character. This is why you, a young black man, gotta work extra hard in the area of getting your education. Not just that, but those manners that Momma be teaching you to use, well, those manners are what's gonna really open up doors for you. Momma taught me when I was your age to respect others and be courteous and all that. But being out here hustling in the streets, one learns to only respect those who have earned it. You, however, don't belong in the streets and as long as I'm alive you're not gonna end up in the streets."

Derrick pulled up to their apartment. "Now promise me one

thing, Mike-Mike."

"What's that, bruh?"

"Promise me that you'll never tell Momma what Veronda did to you. You know she'll kill me if she found out I let you get your little wee-wee wet."

"I promise, bruh, I won't ever say anything about what happened today."

"If you do, I'm not ever gonna do anything special for you again, and I'm serious, Mike."

"Bruh, trust me on this one, I'll never go running my mouth. You can bank on that."

"A'ight, good. I'll see you later when I come back home." Derrick dropped Mike-Mike off and went to make some coke sales.

To be Cond't.

Check out The full novel, The Way It Is, December 15, 2011

Also Check out Death No Exceptions!

Please check out our other books on sale at Amazon and Barnes and Nobles Website for your Kindles and Nooks. Our prices are less than 4.99. We appreciate your support.

Book Sale

Ever bought a good book for 2.99? Here's your chance!!A Big Sale on Books for you Nook, Kindle, Ipads Lovers for a limited time we have some great books on sale!!

Get to know us with this special especially for you. Please check out Prioritybooks Authors on Barnesandnoble.com and Amazon. com. All you have to do is go to www.Amazon.com (kindle Store) or www.BarnesandNoble.com (Nook Store) online stores to download your book.

Also on Kindle and Nook:

Rose Jackson-Beavers:
Backroom Confessions and A Hole in My Heart are on sale for $2.99

Ann Clay: (Romance) Protective Custody, 3.99 A Love for All Times, 3.99 Cupid's Connections, 2.99 Waving from the Heart, 2.99 and Priceless 2.99

Mary L. Wilson- (Urban) Ghetto Luv and Still Ghetto 4.99

**Kareem Tomblin- (Urban) Death No Exceptions 2.99

Stanley Pitchford: (Science Fiction) Destruction via the Mirror (3.99) and Destruction via the Mirror 2 (3.99)

Xavier Pierre, Jr. Lovers Anonymous 1.99

Lady Bea Morgan- (Memoir) The Pastor's Wife Does Cry 4.99

Keisha Ervin- (Urban) Finding Forever 4.99

Jazz Catrell (Urban Erotica) Sex on the Second Floor 2.99

Lydia Douglas Reaching Higher Heights (teens – self-help) 5.99

CPSIA information can be obtained at www.ICGtesting.com
Printed in the USA
LVOW122056161211

259765LV00001B/212/P

9 780983 486046